SPACE ADVENTURES

(Original title: *Teen-Age Space Adventures*)

Edited by

A. L. FURMAN

A LANTERN PRESS BOOK

PUBLISHED BY POCKET BOOKS NEW YORK

SPACE ADVENTURES

Lantern Press edition published January, 1975

L

This POCKET BOOK edition includes every word contained in the original, higher-priced edition. It is printed from brand-new plates made from completely reset, clear, easy-to-read type. POCKET BOOK editions are published by POCKET BOOKS, a division of Simon & Schuster, Inc., 630 Fifth Avenue, New York, N.Y. 10020. Trademarks registered in the United States and other countries.

Standard Book Number: 671-75843-8.
Library of Congress Catalog Card Number: 75-189828.
This Lantern Press edition is published by arrangement with Lantern Press, Inc.

Printed in the U.S.A.

LANTERN PRESS BOOKS

are complete and unabridged reprints of titles in the several series of thematic short-story anthologies published originally by Lantern Press, Inc. Over two million copies have been sold in their higher-priced, cloth-bound editions.

Teachers, librarians, and reviewers have often recommended these carefully edited anthologies. For instance, *Scholastic Teacher* said: "All are suitable as supplementary readers for junior high school students. Each title appears on most school and library approved reading lists and is recommended by *The Library Journal.* Though mainly for junior high school readers, they can be read with pleasure by older students and they are endorsed by Spache in GOOD READING FOR POOR READERS."

A complete list of the titles now available will be found on the reverse side of this page. If your bookseller doesn't have a title you want, you can get it by sending retail price, local sales tax if any, plus 25¢ per book for postage and handling to Mail Service Department, POCKET BOOKS, a Division of Simon & Schuster, Inc., 1 West 39th Street, New York, N.Y. 10018. If you are ordering for delivery in Canada, send retail price plus 25¢ per book for postage and handling to Simon & Schuster of Canada, Ltd., 330 Steelcase Road, Markham, Ontario. In either case, please send check or money order. We cannot be responsible for cash.

Now Available:

Contents

Space Adventures

Total Recall

LARRY STERNIG

THE face of Brian Wargan, chief of the Solar Bureau of Investigation, was gray with strain and fatigue. "This Corvo North business," he said. "It's almost a myth by now, but it's our only chance. We might as well face that."

His features and those of the younger man across the desk from him might have formed a study in contrasts. Roger Kay was keen, alert. There were signs of weariness about his eyes, but the firm set of his jaw revealed a tendency to action rather than introspection.

"Then, sir," he urged, "let's take that chance. The department has located him, I believe? I haven't seen the reports."

The S.B.I. chief nodded. "His laboratory is right here on Gany." He indicated a spot on the global map of Ganymede, some distance from the spaceport.

"That's the mining district," Kay observed.

"Yes. He's been doing some research for the Inter-Planetary Mining Syndicate. We've assigned a special wave band and are in constant communication. Here, I'll introduce you."

Wargan set the dials on the visi-communicator that occupied one corner of his desk; then looked up at the screen on the wall. A blurred rectangle of light flickered and then coalesced into sharpness—and Roger Kay involuntarily drew a deep breath. The girl looking out from the visi-screen was the most beautiful he'd ever seen.

"Is your father making progress, Miss North?" asked Wargan.

The girl on the screen shook her head. "I'm afraid not, Mr. Wargan. He's in the lab now, working, and won't let me disturb him except to bring in coffee and sandwiches. I've been trying to get him to sleep."

"This is Roger Kay, Miss North," said the S.B.I. chief. "One of my assistants. I'm sending him out to your place to see if he can help."

Ann North frowned slightly. "We're doing everything we possibly can already."

"I'm sure of that. But Mr. Kay is rather outstanding as a scientist himself, Miss North. He'll be able to help—at least in some of the detail work, to save time."

Roger Kay grinned. "He means, Miss North, that I can clean the test tubes and solder the wires and let your father save his energy for the brain-work."

His smile was infectious, and the scientist's daughter capitulated. Wargan flicked the switch and threw the screen into blankness.

"I'll give you an order for the fastest helio we have," he said. "You'll be there in three hours. And that means there will be a little less than three days left!"

Roger Kay drew a deep breath, his face suddenly serious. Three days to save the System from an invasion that could not possibly prove to be less than a major catastrophe, less than the end of things as he knew them.

Even now the invaders from Andromeda were approaching the System's outermost defenses; converging upon the virtually helpless garrisons on Pluto. Patrol spacers off the frigid planet had already contacted spearheads of the huge armada—with fatal results.

Once before the System had been periled by these devils from the distant galaxy. Victory had been costly then, but the combined Planetary fleets could not now hope to stave off the full force of this new attack. They would have to yield space; fall back to more favorable positions.

Trionite alone would prove the decisive factor in any war of worlds, and the United Planets had not been able to learn the secret of manufacturing the new explosive, one ton of which could wreck an invading army.

As Roger Kay set the robot-course dial of his

speedy helio for the mining settlement, he switched in for a moment on Wargan's private wave-band. "Leaving now, sir," he reported crisply. "Be there in two hours. Any further instructions?"

"Do your best, Kay, that's all," came the weary voice of the S.B.I. chief. "New reports in confirm the old ones. We expect the first blow by noon Friday. Pluto is doomed; now being evacuated."

"We've got to stop them," Roger Kay said fiercely as he snapped the switch. "We've just got to!"

He settled back to get in a much-needed two hours of sleep while the robot pilot held his course.

The alarm bell awakened him, and he pointed the craft down under the great red disk of Big Jupe, toward the low range of purple cliffs indicated on his map.

A few minutes later he was knocking at the door of the dome-shaped laboratory.

Ann North was twice as beautiful in the flesh as she had seemed on the visi-screen. Attired in the modish shorts and tunic that had become universal garb for Earthwomen, she looked like a figure from a Grecian frieze. She led him to the library.

"Dad's asleep at last," she said. "I persuaded him to rest for a few hours—on the strength of my argument that he'd accomplish more in the long run if he kept his brain clear."

Roger Kay nodded understandingly. "I just had a bit of sleep myself en route. Nobody at headquarters has slept much the last few days. By the way, I'm woefully in the dark about a lot of things. Will you tell me just what your father's trying to rediscover? If you can enlighten me, I'll not have to ask him so many darn-fool questions."

"You know, of course," said Ann North when they were comfortably seated, "that it's a ray that will explode any explosive at a distance. Or perhaps I shouldn't have said a ray—it's really a sound wave, in the ultrasonic belt, traveling on a beam. It disrupts any unstable chemical compound."

Roger Kay nodded. "That much I know. I've examined one of the projectors. We've installed them at all the outposts. They're all ready, except—"

"Except for the catalyst. The part of the discovery that's lost in the chemical compound that produces the catalytic gas. The ultrasonic waves, passing through the gas, change their vibration in some way."

"I see now," said Kay, "why it is directional. The ultrasonic waves go in all directions, of course, but only those passing through the gas are disruptive. Right?"

The girl nodded her beautiful blond head. "It's all very simple, and it's all in the hands of the government, except for the formula for that catalyst. Fortunately my father has a reputation as a scientist. That's why the government was willing to take a chance on having those projectors set up, even though—"

Roger Kay smiled wryly. "Your father is the outstanding scientist of the System, Miss North. But even if he wasn't, we might have taken that chance.

It's about the only chance. If he fails, three days from today—"

"As bad as that?"

"I'm afraid so. But let's not talk about it. One thing I don't know: How was the formula lost?"

"Dad destroyed it. He discovered it accidentally twenty years ago, while working on something else. Never thinking that the fate of worlds might hinge upon it, he destroyed his notes almost as soon as he had made them. He's always been awfully opposed to war, you know, and he saw the terrible possibilities in the weapon if it should fall into the wrong hands."

"That is still true," said a quiet voice from the doorway. Roger Kay recognized Corvo North at once from the many photographs he had seen. He rose and offered his hand.

"I'm glad you're here, Mr. Kay," said the scientist. "Ann told me you were coming. Yes, it's still true that I'm opposed to war—but this isn't war. Even disregarding personal interests and patriotism, it's an attempt to save the human race. Come on into the laboratory. We've no time to waste."

Roger whistled softly under his breath as Corvo North closed the door behind them. The laboratory, spacious and well equipped, was a research worker's dream.

The scientist led the way past rows of pieces of apparatus whose purpose Roger could but dimly guess, to a table at the far end of the room. Upon the table was a small box bristling with dials. The back and top were open, showing a maze of wires and coils and condensers.

"Looks like a radio set with hydrophobia." Roger observed. "What connection has this with the catalyst formula?"

"Nothing, directly. There's no chance, through experimentation, of my recovering that formula in time. Three years, possibly. Three days, never."

"You mean that it's hopeless to try? That the System is lost?" Roger Kay was appalled.

"I don't quite mean that," said North. "But what chance there is lies through this apparatus you're looking at now. Sit down; I'll explain while I work. You can help later, when I've explained the machine."

He began to tinker amidst the maze of wires.

"My discovery of trionite was purely accidental. It was empiric; not based on any theory. There were six or seven chemicals, and I recall the identity of only two of them. The others? Well, count the chemicals in the pharmacopoeia! The only way I could re-discover it would be by accident as I did before—and that would involve too many experiments and too much time. But the formula is buried somewhere in my subconscious mind. I *might* remember it."

Roger Kay eyed the box with some misgivings. "You mean this is—"

"The memory of everything we've ever done or seen is latent in our minds—in the molecular structure of the brain. Almost, I might say, in concentric layers. When the present crisis arose, I had been studying the human brain and the nature of thought and memory. Do you follow me?"

He looked up from his work and as Roger nodded, he saw how haggard and weary was the face of the elderly scientist.

"Consciousness is basically electrical in nature. The act of memory is the shift of that electrical impulse back to a buried stratum of the brain. But the shift is never complete; most of the consciousness stays in the present. We never remember anything perfectly."

"Then this machine is to—"

"To create a magnetic field of such a nature as to shift the consciousness *as a whole*. By shifting the magnetic field's intensity, I can move back the consciousness, or memory, to complete remembrance of any given moment of the past. In other words, under its influence, I hope to send back my memory to the moment when I jotted down the formula. Earlier or later won't do; I didn't memorize it at any time."

His interest completely gripped, Roger Kay stared into the intricate mechanism. "But, sir," he asked, "do you know the exact time that was—down to the minute?"

"Fortunately, yes. I recall that it was the day Ann was being given a party for her third birthday. My wife had told me to be home at three o'clock in the afternoon. I was a little late—didn't leave the lab until on the stroke of three, and it was two or three minutes before then that I wrote down the formula."

"And you think you can hit that exact moment?"

"With a couple of preliminary experiments, yes. If I find that given setting of the dial and the vernier adjustments give me a certain date and time of day, I can calculate the proper adjustment for the time I want."

"Amazing!" exclaimed Roger. "Frankly, if it weren't for the wonderful things you've accomplished in other fields, I'd say it was visionary."

Corvo North shook his gray head. "The theory is sound; it should work. But three days! Man, we're working against a deadly deadline!" He grabbed a pad and pencil. "Here, I'll show you what to do and you can start on the headpiece that connects to the machine here."

And thus started the busiest, dizziest hours of Roger Kay's life. Sleep was a chimera that haunted every leaden-eyed hour, a mirage that beckoned and pleaded in vain.

And the hands of the laboratory clock crept inexorably onward. At three in the morning on Friday, Terran time, with nine hours left before the invaders would strike, Kay staggered to the televis and dialed Wargan.

"I think we'll finish in time," he reported. "We'll be ready for the first test in a couple of hours. Have you made the preparations we suggested?"

The S.B.I. chief nodded. "At the base of each projector we've installed practically a chemical warehouse. There is at least a small quantity of every available known chemical. And expert chemists waiting at each."

"Good. Then within fifteen minutes after I send you the formula, the projectors can be in operation?"

"Ten minutes, unless the formula is more complex than you believe. You say that Corvo North believes there are but six or seven ingredients?"

Roger Kay nodded wearily. "And the communications?"

"Open constantly. An operator on duty at each projector at all times. Test messages going through every fifteen minutes. Incidentally, latest reports still confirm early ones. The deadline is still noon today."

Roger Kay saluted, then snapped the switch. Back to work at the little box in the laboratory.

During those last hours, as well as the ones preceding them, Ann North had been a ministering angel. Sleeping almost as little as the two men, she was ever ready with encouragement—and hot coffee. At times, almost by force, she would pry one or the other of them away from their work for a brief period of rest.

On her own initiative she had called in Dr. Dane. Once he understood the situation, the doctor was invaluable. He took no part in the work on the machine, but he watched over Corvo North constantly and kept him at the highest point of efficiency under the circumstances.

Ten o'clock came—and ten-thirty—and they were ready for the preliminary test.

As he placed the metal plates on his head with shaking hands, Corvo North seemed a mere shell of his former self.

Roger Kay sat at the controls. At North's instructions they ran the wires to an easy chair several yards away, as they were uncertain just how far the magnetic field would extend beyond the headset.

"Better tie me to the chair," North cautioned. "When the field is thrown on, I'll have no recollection of the present or why I'm here. Don't forget that. Until you bring me back by setting the dials to zero, mentally, I'll be back where I was whatever time we hit upon. It will seem to me that I'm waking suddenly in utterly strange circumstances and surroundings. You know what questions to ask, of course."

"Yes, Mr. North," said Roger. He turned to Dr. Dane. "Will you attend to the tying? Just sufficiently so that he can't rise in his bewilderment."

Ann North brought straps, and a few moments later Corvo North nodded that he was ready; then leaned his head back and closed his eyes.

Roger Kay glanced at the instruments and then shifted two of the dials. There was a sudden hum from within the box, and Corvo North's eyes snapped open.

"What—what is this?" he demanded. "Why am I here?"

"Everything's all right, Mr. North," said Roger soothingly. "We'll release you in a moment. First please tell us what is the date."

"It's January twelfth, of course. Why do you—"

"And the year?"

"Twenty forty-five. Now will you kindly—"

"Just one more question, Mr. North. Do you know the exact time of day when you awoke here?"

"How can I when I don't know how I got here? The last thing I remember is walking through the door of the bank to keep my appointment, at nine. What's happened? Did I faint?"

A glow of satisfaction lodged itself in Roger's mind; they were getting the time more accurately than he'd dared expect on the first trial. He pushed his luck a bit farther.

"Were you on time to make that appointment, Mr. North?"

"I'd have been five minutes early. Now will you—"

"Perfect!" exclaimed Roger. He turned back the dials.

Corvo North went limp for an instant, then reopened his eyes. Dr. Dane rushed to him and unbuckled the straps.

"Get anything?" asked the scientist weakly.

"Perfect!" said Roger again. "I've got a note of the exact setting—and you were able to give the time exactly." He scribbled hasty calculations on the pad. "And that setting took you back to January of Twenty forty-five. To be exact—six thousand seven hundred twenty-eight days, twenty-seven hours, seven minutes!"

Corvo North nodded weakly, but excitedly tried to rise. Dr. Dane, his hand on North's pulse, motioned him back.

"That was a tremendous strain on your heart, North," he cautioned. "I forbid you to do it again until you've rested."

"Absurd!" Corvo North glanced at the clock. "There isn't time! It's eleven now!"

"Repeat that again right away and you'll never live to report what you see," warned the physician solemnly. "Half an hour of rest—or the entire experiment will be in vain."

Ann North's face was pale; she looked from her father to Roger Kay pleadingly.

He nodded slowly. "We can just do it. I'll check and recheck the calculations meanwhile—get the dial settings exact. And the next try—Well, it's make or break anyway." His voice was grim. "One more chance, and we get it or we don't."

During that half hour he checked and counter-checked his figures until he was as sure as possible to hit the exact instant in the past—the instant when Corvo North had jotted down the lost formula.

At eleven-thirty, the headset was replaced on Corvo North's head. This time his arms were left free and a pad of paper placed on his lap. His fingers held a pencil. He leaned back and again closed his eyes.

Roger Kay turned the dials.

Corvo North's face tensed, then relaxed. His eyes remained closed. For half a minute, aside from the faint hum from the machine, there was utter stark silence in the laboratory. It was maddening.

Then a faint scratching sound. The others, holding their breath from sheer suspense, saw the pencil in Corvo North's hand begin to move across the pad. Three lines it wrote; stopped.

The formula!

Suddenly the scientist's eyes snapped opened, widened with terror and bewilderment. With a movement so swift that no one could stop him, he ripped the sheet of paper from the pad, crumpled it, and hurled it at the glowing coil of an electric heater!

The paper flashed into flame, crumpled into ash as Corvo North himself crumpled, went limp in the chair.

Roger Kay turned the dials back to zero as Ann and the doctor leaped forward, unstrapped the unconscious scientist. Dr. Dane felt the fluttering pulse, then picked up the frail body and headed for the living quarters. Ann, her blue eyes wide with anxiety, ran ahead to open doors and prepare for the doctor's ministrations.

When she returned, Roger Kay stood before the visi-screen. Ann put a hand on his shoulder. "Dad will be all right," she said, her voice flat with despair, "but we've failed. Dr. Dane says it will be days before he'd dare—"

"Shh," said Roger gently. "Watch." He slipped his left arm around her slim waist, drew her toward the screen.

The vista past the purple range showed at once that the view was eastward from the spaceport. There was no shipping in sight. In the red sky, far out and very high, was a thin silvery line, growing larger.

"The invaders." Unconsciously, Roger Kay whispered rather than spoke. "A thousand spheres at least for us alone. Watch, in a moment we'll know."

"Know what, Roger? Do you mean—"

The visi-screen answered for him. Out there high up in the sky there was a single bright flash—and then a thousand flashes that blended into one blinding one. A roar from the receiver rose to deafening pitch, stopped abruptly.

"Shattered the diaphragm of the transmitter," said Roger quietly. "That was trionite in action, Ann, it's all over. Your father—won!"

"But the formula! He destroyed it!"

Roger Kay put his other arm about her, smiled down. "That was why I was sent here, Ann. To eliminate possible hitches."

"But how—"

"Your father destroyed the formula the first time, and I guessed he might do it again—in his mind he was back some twenty years ago, remember—so I took the elementary precaution of placing carbon paper between the third and fourth sheets of that pad of paper. And I sent Wargan the formula while you were with your father, twelve minutes ago."

A Great Day for the Irish

A. M. LIGHTNER

BRIDGET Kelly stood at the foot of the rocket lift and watched the loading operation. The freight had long since been inspected and stowed, and now it was the passengers' turn. Bridget was glad that for once she was not responsible. Let others worry and snoop. This time she was a passenger herself, starward bound. Inspected, passed and okayed, she could have the pleasure of watching others squirm.

Like that beauty coming aboard with the furs and the orchid. She wouldn't be allowed to keep the orchid, of course. Bridget grinned as she saw the flower tossed into a trash can and imagined the words the beauty was mouthing. The man beside her sported a boutonniere. Yes, there it went into the can. He was still smiling, probably cracking wise. Bridget had separated so many travelers from so many items that she could tell what the passenger was going to say before he said it.

Most people knew that strenuous efforts were being made to keep pests and epidemics away from Earth. Ever since the beginnings of space travel, the quarantine of incoming ships at the Moon had been rigidly observed. But the fact that plagues could also spread *from* Earth seldom registered on the public's mind.

Bridget was all too well aware of it. For several years she had labored to that end in the Quarantine Service. Now that her savings had accumulated and her abilities as an entomologist were recognized, she was about to board one of the shining ships herself. There were raised eyebrows when her destination was known. An entomologist going to New Eden—a planet where insects were at a minimum. But Bridget only smiled. She knew what she wanted. She was bound for the frontier, where men are men and women are scarce.

The speaker blared. The countdown was beginning.

"Fifteen minutes!" rasped the mechanical voice. "Fifteen minutes to blast-off!"

She took a last look at the planet of her birth and squeezed into the lift. The few remaining passengers pushed in with her. A man in a red waistcoat was commiserating with the woman beside him.

"Don't let the officials get you down," he said. "We'll have to put up with them for the journey. But on New Eden, I hear, the conditions are so good they hardly need any regulations at all."

"It isn't that," sniffed his friend. "It's just that you gave it to me and I was hoping to wear it tonight."

"Perhaps I can buy you something in hydroponics. I had no idea they were so touchy or I'd have had the orchid fumigated."

Bridget felt the scorn of the official for the general public. "If you're going to New Eden, you ought to know we want to keep it that way."

The red waistcoat looked down at her.

"Oh, officialdom without stripes?" he said. "Or are you an old hand? Perhaps you can explain the deal before we get there."

So he *was* the type that cracked wise, and she had put her foot in it right at the beginning.

"I've never been off Earth before," she admitted. "I read up on it all first."

The lift was at the lock door, and she slipped through without looking back. The speaker was croaking "Ten minutes to go" as she hurried to her cabin and prepared for takeoff. She'd have to do better than this or the trip would be a washout. Better just concentrate on enjoying it . . . the new experiences . . . the fascination of travel.

The jets roared and Bridget Kelly blacked out.

Several hours later she had recovered enough to spruce up, take the prescribed dose of covitron against space sickness, and make her way to the lounge. She found the table setting with her name on it and had hardly sat down before a familiar voice began at her ear.

"Sure and if it isn't Bridget Kelly, and it's a long time I've been waiting for herself."

She looked up into the same laughing eyes, only this time they were above an emerald-green waistcoat.

"Still determined that New Eden shall not be polluted by snakes? Oh, excuse me, that was St. Patrick. You're worried about bugs."

She laughed in spite of herself and glanced at the place card next to hers. "Mr. Patch Maguire," it read.

"I didn't mean to sound stuffy," she said. "It's just that most people don't realize how important it is . . . how much trouble just a few insects . . . well, I've worked at it and I ought to know."

"Ah, an official entomologist. But in that case, why New Eden? Or are you insurance against people like Carrie and me who might import something?"

"You never can tell. Something may turn up. It's hard to imagine a planet without any insects at all."

"Eden's remarkable that way," put in the young officer sitting across from them. "No stinging bugs or parasites. Makes everything a lot more comfortable. Still, it's pretty new. Only a small part developed so far."

"So we've insurance against the unknown in Bridget Kelly."

"And what might *you* be insurance against, Mr. Maguire?" she countered.

The officer stared. "Don't you folks know each

other? Mr. Maguire's a grower of fancy plants. Sort of goes together . . . plants and insects!" He laughed. "Well, it looks like the rest of our table won't show up for this meal."

"What happened to the lady without the orchid? She was with you, wasn't she?" Bridget asked.

"Carrie," said Patch Maguire, "is one of those unfortunates on whom covitron does not work. She won't be with anyone for the duration. I was just hoping our whole table was not similarly afflicted."

"It's a pity," mused the young officer. "So many people make the flight across space only once. If they did it more often, they might get accustomed."

"Don't you take covitron?" Bridget asked, beginning to wonder how soon she should repeat the dose. Some people said it made you sleepy, and she certainly didn't want that with things just getting started . . . and Patch Maguire . . . Patch Maguire . . .

Suddenly a window opened in her mind. She saw a letter with short punching sentences. "You think you can get away with this high-handed, overbearing, totally uncalled-for destruction of property? I'll take it to the top! I'll see you idiots in hell . . . or at least out of the Service!" Patch Maguire protesting the destruction of his shipment of seeds imported from Regulus V. No amount of explanation that the seeds had been found to harbor a blight which, once let loose on Earth . . . Patch Maguire had a reputation as an authority on crossbreeding and mutation of plants . . . and also for throwing his weight around. It was several years ago, but Bridget remembered the consternation in the department.

She realized that Maguire and the officer were talking. They were agreeing that space sickness was only a matter of psychology, and that if you just didn't think about it, no covitron was necessary. She hastily swallowed another pill with her coffee and hoped the coffee would keep her awake.

They toured the ship together, she and Patch. They marveled at the scene from the viewport and chatted with the captain in the control room. The steward inquired about his taste in music and stereo, and he even gave advice to the gardeners in hydroponics. All doors were open to Patch, and there were murmurs about the "handsome couple" as they moved through the lounge. By the end of the trip they were making plans for New Eden. Patch insisted that Bridget was in the wrong profession and she agreed that the science of agriculture might be more rewarding than entomology under certain conditions.

At the farewell dinner, Patch gave her a bouquet he'd had made up especially by the gardeners. But she was more interested in the small green leaf he wore in his lapel. He took it out and insisted on fastening it in her hair.

"Sure and it's a shamrock!" he cried, as he arranged it. "And have you forgotten what day it is tomorrow?"

"It's the day we land," Bridget replied. "But what

day that is in our time or ship's time . . . it's too confusing!"

"It's St. Patrick's Day, that's what it is!" he said. "A great day for the Irish and a great day for us. And I wouldn't be without the shamrock on St. Patrick's Day! They should call the planet New Ireland, that they should. Wasn't Ireland the garden island, all green and fruitful and with no snakes? And I hear this planet's the garden planet and with no insects either to make life miserable. But let you and me be living there a while and we'll make it New Ireland for sure!"

And he planted a kiss on her mouth without a thought of who was looking at them.

As their tablemates drank to their health, Bridget blushed and her eyes shone, and after dinner Patch escorted her to the stereo where they sat very close together in the dark. But as the pictures flashed across the screen and as Patch's arm went across her shoulder and drew her close, her mind was besieged by an army of little doubts. Shamrock . . . shamrock . . . what had she read about the shamrock?

"Patch," she whispered. "Where did you get it?"

"Get what?" Patch murmured, bending over to kiss her.

"The shamrock, Patch? I don't believe they have it in hydroponics."

"Sure, they must have it." Patch's lips brushed hers and she found it difficult to think clearly.

"I never saw it there. Patch! Are you sure?"

"Saw what? I don't see anything but you. That's enough for me."

"About the shamrock, Patch!"

"It looks beautiful on you. Sure and I wouldn't be without a shamrock on St. Patrick's Day."

Bridget gave up. She lay back in the sanctuary of his arm and basked in the warm feeling of his lips on her hair. But the doubts kept crawling about in her mind. What was the matter with her? Couldn't she be happy when everything was perfect? Had she been a cut-and-dried inspector for too many years? But she remembered the words of Professor Schwarzkopf, the day she received her degree: "The inspectors are the watchdogs of the planets. Without them, all that man has built can be destroyed."

When Patch had kissed her good night outside her cabin and his footsteps had died away along the corridor, she crept out into the passage and made her way to hydroponics.

"Why, no," said the chief gardener, "we never carry clover of any sort. Why do you ask?"

On her way to the control room, Bridget tried not to think. She found the young officer from her table on duty with the captain, and the two men listened in surprise as she outlined her fears.

"I don't want to accuse Mr. Maguire of anything," she said. "I'm sure he doesn't realize how serious—and of course there may be nothing to it. It's just that I remember that shamrocks harbor the golden nematode—that is, in the soil around the roots. And it seems likely that if Mr. Maguire has live shamrocks—and I remember what a serious plague they once brought over from Ireland to America . . ."

The captain pulled his mustache. "It's clearly against regulations. I can't imagine how he'd get it past inspection. But then, Maguire's a very persistent man and he's got pull in odd places. I don't want to rouse the ire of the Irish, but I see your point."

"Couldn't you search his cabin—without his knowing I said to? Oh, I'm sure he'd be very angry. But if I could only look at his plants, then I'd be sure if they're safe. You must have ways of getting in—if there should be a short circuit or something in his cabin."

"Oh, we have ways," the captain said. "Don't we, Lieutenant?"

"Perhaps at breakfast," suggested the young officer. "If Miss Kelly could arrange to make it as leisurely as possible."

"And right afterward you might go to the lieutenant's cabin—with your instruments and without Mr. Maguire."

She had no trouble in making her breakfast leisurely. She could hardly choke it down. Under Patch's admiring gaze and flagrant approval she was uncomfortably conscious of treachery. She left as soon as the protracted meal was over, even though she knew it would give him the opportunity to discover the rape of his plants.

The lieutenant was waiting for her in his cabin.

He sat behind his desk eyeing a motley collection of clover in an assortment of little jars and boxes. Bridget brought out her pocket scope and without a word pulled the first specimen up by the roots and began to examine it. The lieutenant watched in fascination.

"It's a good thing Mr. Maguire can't see you now," he said. "He'd take an entirely different tone from the one I've been hearing lately."

"I'm hoping he doesn't find out," she muttered. "What he doesn't know . . . Oh! Oh! Look here! A fine big cyst! Now if they're all like this . . ."

The lieutenant's face took on a look of respect. He came around from behind his desk and peered over her shoulder. "Found something already?" he asked.

Bridget pushed the scope under his nose. "See that?" she said. "In the right-hand corner."

"You mean that lump? Doesn't look very dangerous."

"No, it doesn't. But it's a nematode cyst, all right. That little brown lump, if turned loose in the soil—give it a few years and you'll have a real pest on your hands."

"You don't say. We'd better get rid of it right away. Do you think there's any more?"

"That's just what I'm going to find out."

But before she could move to the desk for the other containers there was a sound of scuffling outside, the door was flung violently open, and a rich, Irish voice proclaimed in righteous anger: "So here you are, conspiring against me! Both the culprits red-handed! And my shamrocks, my little plants, my babies! Thank heavens I got here in time!"

The lieutenant moved to intercept him. "I beg your pardon, sir, but these plants are in quarantine, and if you have any others we haven't found—"

"You're no true daughter of Ireland, Bridget Kelly. And I'm fortunate to have found you out in time, false and faithless as you are!"

"Now, now," cautioned the lieutenant, getting between Maguire and the desk. "She was only doing her duty. You should see the things she's been showing me in her microscope. A menace to the whole planet!"

"Don't you believe a word of it!" thundered Maguire. "These inspectors are full of fears and fancies. Puffed up with their own importance. And I'll thank you to give me back my plants that you stole out of my cabin."

"I'm afraid I can't do that," the lieutenant said. "Not until Miss Kelly has examined each one—and then only the ones that get a clean bill of health." And he began to collect the little pots and remove them as far as possible from Maguire's reach.

"Well, come along then, Bridget—give them the bill of health," Maguire ordered. "You'll do that for me, I'm sure. And I don't know what all the fuss is about either, all over a few little plants, and shamrocks at that."

"The few little plants have a few little cysts all through their roots," said Bridget, whose temper was wearing thin. "I've only looked at one so far, but as nice an infestation of the golden nematode I've seldom seen. It's got to go down the incinerator."

"The incinerator!" screamed Maguire. "Woman! My shamrocks! All the way from Ireland!"

"If you hadn't spent your whole life circumventing regulations and pulling strings, this wouldn't have happened. Why didn't you get them treated and certified before coming aboard?"

"Because there wasn't time, that's why!" Patch shouted. "They only came from Ireland as I was leaving for the ship. If it hadn't been for a snooping, sniveling worrywart—all about a worm that you can't even see . . ."

"You can see the results right enough!" Bridget's voice was rising to match his. "Did you ever hear of the Long Island potato? The best on the East Coast they were. The golden nematode ruined Long Island for potatoes. That's what the shamrock did for America! That's a sneaking, treacherous worm for you!"

"And who would want to grow potatoes on Long Island, built up into a city as it is?"

"They're going to want to grow potatoes on New Eden, and I'm here to see they can."

"If that's all that's worrying you, I'll breed you a nematode-resistant potato. And now I'll thank you to let me take my shamrocks and make an end to this disgraceful scene."

But when he looked around, he found the lieutenant had quietly removed himself with the plants, and the door of the cabin was crowded with interested passengers.

"So you think you've put one over on me!" Patch shouted. "It's a good thing I found out in time how I was being deceived by a pair of eyes and a mouth that says one thing and means another!"

"And I suppose you're the soul of honor! With no thought of responsibility to your fellow man! You've had your way all your life, and it's lucky I found *that* out, too—before—before . . ."

But he was gone, elbowing his way through the crowd, and the onlookers drifted away, embarrassed at the sight of the stormy girl who shouted hysterically after him. Bridget slammed the door and collapsed into a chair.

"I'm sorry for the noise," she apologized when the officer returned. "I'd better finish checking the plants before it's time to land."

"Never mind the plants," the lieutenant told her. "I've put them where he won't find them in a hurry. As a matter of fact, we aren't going to land. We're in orbit now and they're to send a rocket shuttle. They aren't worried about what we're bringing in this time. It's what we might take out. There's a howling plague on New Eden after all. Several of our passengers have changed their minds about landing."

"A plague?" said Bridget stupidly. It was hard to concentrate on anything more deadly than the golden nematode.

"Oh, nothing you or I could catch. Something to do with agriculture and the plants. Which reminds me, I've a batch of telegrams for you. The authorities are delighted to learn we've a registered entomologist aboard. Very few of them have come this way."

By the time Bridget had read the sheaf of papers, she had made the transition from the world of shipboard romance to her accustomed world of science and order. There was work to be done. Her talents were needed in a dozen places at once. She left orders for the confiscated clovers to be destroyed and went to her cabin to pack. She was on the first shuttle to leave the ship.

The weeks that followed were filled with hard work with test tube and microscope, at her desk and in the field. The majority of her co-workers were men, but none had time to look for a laughing eye or a smiling mouth. The beautiful garden planet of New Eden was being reduced to a desert by a mysterious *something* that was swiftly attacking all the cultivated areas. Starvation was looming and there was talk of hasty evacuation. The situation was passing out of control.

The villain could not be isolated. Was it an insect, a virus, a chemical in the soil? Some of the few native insects were caught and subjected to experiment. The soils were analyzed and tested. Those were not the answer. The only thing certain was that the previously lush brown loam was turning to a yellow, chalky sand, and everything that grew in it withered and died.

Bridget visited farm after farm and trudged from field to field. She looked at worried faces and tried to think of words of encouragement. Back at the laboratory she studied her specimens far into the night and fell asleep at her desk. She was too tired to think about Patch Maguire, who, she concluded, had never left the spaceship. What would a grower of gardens, a breeder of plants do in a spreading desert? He had gone on to some more flourishing planet.

She was called to the office one day.

"I hear there's a farm that claims they don't have the plague," said the harassed young scientist behind the desk. "Better get over there and see if it's any more than a rumor. Take the heli and bring back all the usual samples. Here's the directions on getting there."

He shoved a torn piece of paper at her and turned back to his cluttered desk. Bridget picked up her collecting kit and climbed into the cab of the machine. By this time she knew her way about the settlements. Without doubt, she told herself, this farm was on the outskirts of civilization, in some valley as yet untouched by the plague. But long before she reached the limits of cultivated land, she could see her destination. It stood out like an oasis in the desert, a little patch of green between a dried-up cornfield and an expanse of stricken wheat.

Bridget brought her heli down on a velvety lawn

in front of a small cottage and walked, unbelieving, to the door. A shout from within welcomed her and she entered a clean and simple kitchen-parlor. The owner of the one healthy farm in New Eden was busy in the attached greenhouse.

As she glimpsed the red waistcoat dangling from a hook, Bridget screamed, and Patch Maguire came through the greenhouse door, a flower pot in one hand, trowel in the other.

"And if it isn't the worm-hunter herself!" he cried. "The czar of the spaceways! The dandelion dictator! And I was wondering how long it would take you to find me out."

"But you—" she gasped. "You couldn't—you wouldn't—aren't supposed to be here!"

"And why not?" he countered. "I'm not like Carrie, she'd rather go on too sick to eat in space than face starvation on this planet. And then the bargain I was offered for this place—you wouldn't believe it! All modern conveniences and they were practically giving it away. Besides, what had I to fear with the best entomologist in five solar systems working for the Department of Agriculture? Sure, you'll be having the problem solved in no time!"

"Don't be giving me that blarney!" Bridget said. "You need only look out the window to know we've solved nothing at all. And you're sitting here crowing to yourself! You've been breeding plague-resistant plants, that's what you've done, and keeping them all to yourself! It's a disgrace!"

Patch began to laugh, and the more he laughed, the angrier Bridget got.

"You should be ashamed!" she shouted. "The whole planet dying and you're sitting here growing greener all the time!"

"And that's the way it's been," he assured her. "This place was dying on me, too. But only the last few days it's taken a new lease and I'm at my wit's end to explain it."

"You mean you don't *want* to explain it. You're hoarding the secret, and it's a shameful thing!"

"Woman, you're crazy!" he bellowed at her. "I'm no magician to breed a plague-resistant plant overnight. It takes patience and many seasons, and I've only just settled in. I put a few things in the garden and stirred things up in the potting shed. Here, come along—you can see for yourself."

He drew her through the cottage, pointing out the advantages of the kitchen so near the greenhouse. She walked about the paths and felt of the rich brown soil without a streak of yellow, and finally her eyes fell upon some little low leaves by the back step.

"Patch," she demanded, "what's that?"

"You've the eagle eye, to be sure. What do you suppose it is?"

"It's clover," she said. "Shamrock to you. Surely not the same shamrock! I gave strict orders!"

Before he could stop her, she had tugged a plant

up by the roots and pulled out her pocket microscope as she bent over it.

"Sure, they were so busy worrying about the plague here, they forgot all about the little plague from Earth. And all I wanted was a bit of old Ireland to bring with me. A few little cysts couldn't be that important. And you've got to admit that's what I've got—a green island!"

"The idiots!" screamed Bridget. "The irresponsible, shirking, doublefaced—"

Her hand went up and Patch dodged involuntarily, expecting her to throw shamrock, dirt and all right at his head. But her hand stopped in midair.

"Patch!" Her voice fell to a whisper of incredulity. "I think I've got the answer here in my hand. Don't say a word till I'm sure, but get me soil samples from all over your place—there—and over there—and *hurry!*"

Patch ran back and forth with the soil samples and Bridget looked in her microscope, and everywhere the golden nematode was teeming and nowhere was there a sign of the sinister yellow streaks.

"Don't you see?" Bridget said. "Whatever it is, the nematodes are killing it."

"It will take some experimenting to prove it, but Bridget, my girl, I believe you're right."

"And while they're proving it, Patch, you and I are going to breed nematodes right here."

And she had a vision of the golden horde, burrowing from Patch's land in all directions, bringing back health and sanity to the land. Whatever would Professor Schwarzkopf say? Dear Professor Schwarzkopf! Sometimes the watchdogs are too faithful. They keep out everyone—even our friends.

And that was how New Eden was saved. And the nematodes prospered and the Maguires prospered and the shamrocks grew everywhere. And so there was nothing for it but to call the planet New Ireland.

Master Race

RICHARD ASHBY

ONE moment he was piloting a fast plane over dangerous green jungles . . . and the next Eddie was wide awake and peering through the gloom. Across the room Rags was whining softly and sniffing the damp night air that rolled in through the open window. The Scotty was excited, Eddie saw, and it must be something out of the ordinary for Rags' whimpering carried an undercurrent of perplexity and fear . . . and the dog wasn't a coward.

The boy called softly to him, but Rags, after tossing back a swift glance of recognition, put his forefeet up on the sill and peered, muttering, out across the pastures.

Eddie slipped from his bed and padded over to the window. As he comfortingly ruffed the fur behind the Scottie's ears, he listened intently at the night. At first he heard only the ordinary country sounds—roosters crowing over at the next farm, the muffled thumping of stock shifting about in the barn and against the corral fence; the flittering and high chirping of birds in the cottonwoods and pepper trees. He took the dog in his arms and was about to go back to bed with him when he became aware of a sound that was very much out of the ordinary. A sound, Eddie decided, something like standing outside the church in Riverside when the organist was playing low, vibrant notes inside.

Eddie wondered how he could have first missed the sound, so firmly had it now become established. Where could it be coming from? It was, he guessed, about an hour till dawn, and no tractors or other farm machinery should be running. And it wasn't a radio.

A plane?

Leaning from the window he glanced upwards, then gasped in astonishment. Goose pimples of excitement tingled his skin, for there in the sky, above the oak tree on the ridge hung a pattern of sharp white lights. They were little lights, as if someone had strung together a fanciful arrangement of Christmas tree bulbs, then sent them dangling aloft beneath a kite.

Rags' mutterings became deep and angry. Finally he gave vent to a short sharp bark.

Instantly Eddie quieted the dog. Lights or not, his mother had made it plenty clear about Rags' being in the house.

Crouching on the floor, both arms about Rags, Eddie whispered words of reassurance while he stared up at the strange sparklings. The oak tree—the one with his tree house—was a scant quarter mile from where he knelt, and he wondered if its being so high on the ridge had caused it to draw some sort of lightning to itself. He'd read of that happening . . . chain lightning. Or was it called Fox Fire? Eddie couldn't remember. Anyway, it looked something like that, he imagined.

But no lightning, he remembered, made a noise like a machine. Unconsciously, he'd hooked sight and sound together.

Frowning, Eddie let go of the dog. If the lights had been over the barn or garage, he'd have gone to tell his father. Or over the garden, his mother. But the tree house didn't concern them. It was his, and even if it hadn't been an hour before dawn he wouldn't have told his parents. He had things in there he shouldn't have, and it wouldn't do for either mother or father to go snooping around, even if they couldn't find his secret ladder and climb it.

He returned to the window.

Something thrashed in the highest branches of the oak. Rags began his whining again.

There was but one thing to do. He found his moccasins by the night table, pulled them on, and threw a leather jacket on over his pajamas. From the wall above his desk, Eddie took down his .22, broke it, slipped in a shell, and tiptoed from the house.

The humming was stronger outside. Not louder, exactly, but more easy to feel. He crouched down, the way he'd seen commandos do in pictures, and began to run, holding the rifle at ready before him. And for once, Rags seemed content to stay at his side and not go dashing along ahead up the path. As they took the turn by the big rock a startled night-bird plunged out of the bushes and took wing. The bird's violent rush brought caution to Eddie and he slowed his run to a walk. Suppose, he thought, that someone in a helicopter or maybe a balloon was hanging over the tree house. Spies, probably. And suppose they wanted the tree house for a headquarters.

He stopped, looked back down at the house dimly outlined in the starlight. Suppose, he continued, that there were too many of them. He'd just better sneak up quietly and see what was going on.

He eased himself around another turn in the path and came again in view of the oak. The lights were still there, but they no longer looked to be mere points of brightness against an empty sky. He stopped, more puzzled than ever . . . they looked like navigation lights on a ship, and a couple of them like the glow from inside a radio. And all of them were swaying gently in the night wind, twenty feet or so above the tree.

Rags went slowly ahead, two feet, three, four, then stopped . . . belly almost to the dust. His teeth shone in a soundless snarl, not a muscle of his body moving. Eddie had never seen him act like this, not even when the bear had come down into the valley to raid for chickens. Rags was plainly terrified, and something of the dog's emotion communicated itself. The boy bit his lip grimly, then strained to listen, heard what the dog was hearing; someone . . . something was moving about up in the oak.

Some of his fear gave way to anger. "Messin' around in my tree house!"

He gripped the rifle tightly, took two determined steps forward. The third step he never completed. He was unconscious when he pitched into the ground. And when Rags leaped after him, he too crumpled as if dead . . .

The Commander left his report-strewn desk and strode heavily over to the forward port. Glumly, he looked down at the frosty pitted surface of the satellite a thousand miles away, and in his imagination saw the planet that swung on the dead orb's opposite side. It was nonsense to have to hide behind a moon from such a primitive planet, waiting and waiting like a coward for reassuring information. But such prudence had ever been part of holy Law.

He sighed, turned away from the huge wall of window. Sometimes one wondered about Law, he mused darkly. One did not disobey, of course, but one could not help wondering sometimes. And occasionally one even wondered the blackest heresy of all—was it really important to kill all life everywhere for the sake of colonization.

The Commander caught sight of his reflection in

a polished door panel. His own hard eyes glowered out from the reflection accusingly, so he pulled up his shoulders and put all suspicion from his mind. Would he not destroy any of his people for such thoughts? Then he must not allow himself to entertain such blasphemy. Naturally, colonization was all-important. That was Law.

Picking up the pictures taken when they had first flashed into this system, the Commander saw again the nature of the beings they were about to exterminate. That they were ignorant savages, quite unworthy of the usual precautions now being taken, was plain to see. Their atmosphere showed heavy traces of carbon combustion, a certain indication that the creatures were inefficient, for who but a savage would burn matter to obtain power? The amount of radioactivity present in their gaseous envelope was so tiny as to prove that they had little or no knowledge of atomic power. There were no *frell* vibrations apparent; imagine existing without an understanding of simple magnetics!

He picked up an enlargement of one portion of a land mass, put a hand magnetic lens over it. The magnification showed clusters of dwellings, linked together by lines and double lines upon the ground —certainly the ultimate proof of low-order civilization, when beings chose to live clustered together, commuting by land, when they could spread themselves out over the surface of their planet and use the roads of the sky.

The Commander made a sign in the air with his

fingers and a door popped open at the end of the vast room. An aide ran toward the desk, halted, covered his face in salute.

"Sir?"

"How long has the scout been gone?"

The aide removed his hands from his eyes. "A day and a night, sir. He should be back any time, now."

"Fool!" The Commander roared out the word. "Did I ask for your guesses? I know he's due back. He is, in fact, one hour overdue." He did not know if this was or was not true, but it was good discipline policy. "Lock him away when he arrives."

The other covered his face respectfully. "Yes, sir." He turned, ran from the desk and out the door.

For a few minutes the Commander kept busy by calling the ten ray-centers of the three-mile-long ship, demanding to know if they were ready to beam. They were. He then spent a while ordering all unit leaders to hold their sections in readiness for inertialess drive. The unit leaders protested politely that they were. He called engine, commanded that they "look sharp." Meekly they assured him that all was well.

With only small satisfaction, the Commander rose from his desk, paced slowly over to the port again. As he gazed out at the moon's bland surface, he reflected that there was something about this nine planet system they were in that made him edgy . . . made him want to keep active and alert.

And where was that thrice-blasted scout?

He decided to have him flogged when he returned. Good discipline policy.

The Scout woke from his drunken sleep and glanced at the clock on the dash of his little craft. It was very late, he saw. He would have to think of a fine excuse when he returned or they would put him in Truth and learn that all Scouts took the precious freedom of voyages to become intoxicated for a while.

Not much time! He would have to take what he could find in the vicinity. Small difference it made, though, since the beings of the planet were surely doomed.

The Scout yawned, then lifted the ship from the mountain and arrowed it down into the folds of the valley. His visor translated the immediate night into light, showing him the typically repugnant surface features of a type J planet: Foliage, sharp young geology, water flowing in natural beds. A world like a hundred others he'd visited in the name of Law.

When the floor of the valley came up he leveled off, then silently sped along in search of dwellings. Beneath him, on level stretches of land, stood odd four-legged creatures. The dominants of this world? he wondered. Probably not. The extremities of their limbs appeared to be too blunt and crude to do even the simple tooling he'd noticed during his flight in. Beasts of transport, no doubt. Boldly, he swooped low over a group, scattering them in panic.

The meadow ended with almost sheer mountain wall, and the Scout whipped his craft up its face and down the opposite side. Something flickered in his vision screen and he swung the controls. A dwelling! In a moment he was back over it, hanging motionless. Sure enough, a revolting crude shack that nestled high in the branches of one of this world's surface growths.

This was it. There was no time nor need to search further.

He locked the controls, then turned on the deadly screen that would kill all life directly beneath, save one properly shielded such as himself, and would stun all life attempting to enter the edges of the field.

Pulling on his helmet, the Scout reached to the stud at his belt and reduced his weight to but a fraction of itself. Then he opened the hatch and clambered out into the air.

His first few minutes of exploration in the tree house were disappointing. There was no life, no corpses about for him to dissect and study. But the hunting club puzzled him. Obviously tooled by machinery and scuffed from much killing, it bore what might be a word burnt into its thickened end: "SPAULDING." He realized he was in an extremely primitive section of the planet, for this weapon was, no doubt, a trade article from some more advanced portion of the globe. Too bad he'd had to land in this region. Dull.

The club he chucked into the bag over his shoulder.

A round object, made of some fairly soft material, with seams twisting over its surface next caught his eye. He took it up, shook it. It, too, bore the symbol "SPAULDING." Probably a totem word. Perhaps the sign of this particular tribe. He put it with the club. It was followed by a small package of soft white cylinders which were stuffed with crumbles of dried weed. Each cylinder bore the sign "CAMEL" as did the container, which also showed a beast, somewhat like those he had buzzed.

And beyond that there was nothing.

A simple people indeed, he pondered. He was about to leave when he noticed the stack of artifacts in one corner. The Scout bent to examine them. They seemed to be composed of the same material as the white of the "CAMEL" cylinders, but thicker and bound together in long wide flat construction. There were bright colors on the outside of each, and just as he discovered that the individual leaves of material could be separated and turned, the alarm bell sounded twice in his helmet. Life had blundered into the outer edges of his field.

Hastily, the Scout put a score of his latest finds into his sack and left the tree house. And without bothering to search for the life that had triggered his alarm (Law specified a Scout was to flee in such an instance) he adjusted his weight and rose up to his waiting ship.

Minutes later he had passed the world's satellite and was in view of his parent craft.

The Commander's first action was to order the Scout flogged before his comrades as an example of what awaited those who became lax in the performance of important duties. His second was to assemble the Council of Experts. When the eight old men had taken their places about the table, the Commander saluted them in the name of Law, then summoned his aide. "Is Decontamination through?"

"It is, sir."

"Then have the findings brought in."

The officer ran from the room and returned in a moment with the Scout's bulging sack. Gently he placed it in the center of the round table before the council. After saluting he took his leave again.

"Gentlemen," began the Commander, "we are met again to pass judgment on a corrupt, life-harboring planet. By the authority vested in me through the line of my father I charge you with the voice of Law." And so on, and on, with the ancient words of the ritual. The eight old experts hardly listened. They had sat through countless identical sessions during the hundreds of years of their lives. Theirs was but to view the oddities that would presently be arranged before them, make mental records of their descriptions, and offer one or two tentative guesses as to the nature of the articles. But in any event, the action that followed would be the same. The creatures responsible for the articles would shortly be snuffed out . . . in the glorious and awful name of Law.

So they hardly listened.

When the Commander had finished with the rites of the occasion he unsnapped the bag and after peering within it, gingerly brought out the Scout's first find. Only now did the old men appear to take much notice. A few even leaned forward slightly. All eyes centered on what their Commander held.

"A phallic object?" asked the youngest.

"No. A lever," said the eldest.

"For killing," added the next.

"But it was made by machine," put in a fourth.

For a moment they were silent. The Commander placed the "machine-made killing-lever" on the table. It described a short little halfroll, bringing the printing into view.

"A religious design," said the youngest. "Obviously pagan."

"But rather well worked."

No one found anything further to say, so the Commander brought forth from the bag the next object. A mild flurry of interest ensued when it was discovered that this soft globular thing bore the same "religious design." But the sages would not venture an opinion as to the thing's purpose, so the Commander took out the package of white cylinders.

Only the next to the eldest made any comment. He claimed that he had seen such articles in his youth, brought out from a system of three worlds that swung above a nova. The white things there, he reminisced, were units of value . . . useful in bartering. They were designed to be spent quickly, lest the stuffing fall out. The other experts agreed that these were no doubt also monies.

The Commander had been listening with but half an ear. Privately, he had long considered the experts to be but a muttering pack of senile dolts . . . dead weight, useless cargo on the ship. They worked not, neither did they breed. But Law demanded their presence. The Law, he mused, seemed strange at times.

He discovered the Council was waiting for him. Frowning to cover his embarrassment, he took out the last of the Scout's finds. For a moment all of them were struck by the bright colors on the flat surface. Then one old man reached out a trembling hand. "Records," he murmured incredulously. "Records such as our own race is said to have once made, long long ago before Law." Reverently, he examined the cover, then with remarkable agility for one so decrepit he jumped to his feet and flung the thing from him. His face twitched with horror.

The others, shocked and disbelieving, fell to examining the rest of the new articles. In a moment, cries of alarm filled the council room. Chairs were upset, dignity forgotten. Only the eldest retained his composure, although with difficulty, for he could hardly manage to control the palsied shaking of his hands. The astonished Commander leaned over his shoulder and watched as the ancient turned the pages.

What he saw made the blood drum in his ears, made his vision swim, and only faintly did he hear the old one's croaking words. "Praise to Law, which we so carelessly accepted, for Law has saved us from the fiendish denizens of this planet. Had we attempted to exterminate them, their space armadas would have taken instant revenge. For they are obviously mightier than we." He put down the bright record of space craft vaster than the one which they occupied and took up another. On its cover was depicted a world being blasted into flaming wreckage, and within was shown the pictorial history of a space fleet, engaged in repelling an alien invasion, and who followed up their successful repulse by annihilating the entire system of the aliens.

Five more of the record books did they examine before the Commander's stunned mind at last reeled beneath the hideous concepts and he could look no more. Dumbly, he managed to reach the phones and order the ship thrown into emergency drive to some far and lost point in space and dimension.

And as he waited for the shuddering wrench that signalled interdimensional shift, he tried to forget the horrors they had so narrowly escaped: Creatures who could make themselves invisible, who had mastered space travel, who worked in magic more powerful than that of Law's, who could whiff out entire solar systems, who could survive incredible mishaps and hardships. Creatures who were no less than Gods!

A wave of fear tore at the Commander as the glittering moon faded away. Eternal nothingness of grey enclosed the ship . . .

The sun was up when Eddie recovered consciousness. Stiff and cold, he sat and looked around sleepily a moment before remembering. Then, as he saw Rags sitting before him, tail wagging happily, it all began to come back: Last night, sometime; humming lights above the tree house, someone moving about up there, himself sneaking up to see, then . . . nothing. He must have tripped and knocked himself out, somehow. Eddie snatched up the .22 and aimed it at the tree. "Whoever's up there," he said, getting to his feet, "had better come on out!"

Nothing happened.

Eddie bent down cautiously, his eyes still fixed on the tree house, picked up a rock and hurled it through the shanty's open door. A bird fluttered from the gnarled oak, sailed across the morning meadow chirping angrily.

"This is your last chance. Come on out, or I'm comin' up and get you!" The bird's being there made him quite sure that everything was all right, so after a moment he pulled the knotted rope from its concealment in a cleft of the tree and went up hand over hand.

A strange odor lingered inside the shack. Something like . . . Eddie sniffed, frowned . . . something like a freshly blown fuse, but outside of that nothing seemed amiss at first. Then he discovered his softball and bat were missing. He found he didn't care too much. The season was over anyway; and besides, hunting and riding and fishing were more fun.

He looked further.

The cigarettes! He hoped the thief wouldn't snitch on him to dad. But that didn't make too much sense, he realized. The thief . . . a tramp, probably, was far away by now, maybe at this very minute trying to trade the ball and bat for a meal or a drink.

And those humming lights? Even now he wasn't too sure he'd seen them. Stars, probably. The Little Dipper, or maybe fireflies, or lightning. Sure.

He turned to go. The sun told him it was almost seven o'clock. Mother would be furious if she found him out in the morning without having dressed properly, or eaten.

It was then he saw that something else was missing, but because it was so late he didn't stop to worry. "Mandrake The Magician," "The Invisible Boys," "Buck Rogers," "Bat Man" . . . they were all old comic books. He'd finished with them months ago.

Eddie clambered down the rope, and seconds later he and Rags were joyfully racing along the trail that led to home.

It was a beautiful morning.

Fateful First Day on Xene

ARTHUR TOFTE

IN spite of himself, Jon Eldon felt a growing sense of excitement . . .

The big starship, Aleron, had come in—Aleron, the eagle. Almost two hundred feet tall, it stood now in all its shining brilliance on the landing pad.

Jon—a stocky, sandy-haired, well-muscled lad of average height—stood with the others watching the passengers disembark. One by one they came down the mechanical chair lift from the open hatchway far overhead.

In his hands Jon nervously held a card on which was lettered a big 17. Looking down on it now, he wished that he really was seventeen. Actually he was three months short of that age. Somehow he had the feeling that reaching the age of seventeen would be the most important thing that could ever happen to him.

Right now his task was to spot the passenger

whose number matched his own. According to advance information, there were supposed to be twenty-four boys and six girls. Jon shuddered at the thought that he might be stuck with a girl.

Before the arrival of the ship, he had overheard two of his friends saying they wished they could get girls to show around.

Not him! He wanted no part of being nursemaid to a weak, sniveling girl. Life on Xene was hard enough without a girl tagging along wherever he went. He couldn't imagine, for instance, taking a girl into the old deserted mine tunnel he had just discovered. It would be a lot more fun to have another boy with him, a boy with the same spirited sense of adventure that he had.

As the passengers, one by one, reached the ground, they paused for a moment. Then they would take a shaky step or two as though testing their land legs. Finally they would hold up their numbered cards. Anxiously they peered at the welcoming crowd, looking for their matching numbers.

Jon suddenly gave a start. Number 17 had just stepped out of the chair lift. Was it a boy or a girl? All dressed alike in space suits.

He reached around for his breather bottle and took a deep whiff of pure oxygen. He wanted to be fully alert when he met his matching number. It was to be his job to spend the next several days introducing that person to the strange ways of Xene. If only it were not a girl!

As Number 17 turned in his direction, Jon's heart suddenly sank. Just his luck. It was a girl!

Gritting his teeth to hide his disappointment, he pushed his way through the crowd and walked up to the girl holding the 17 card.

"I'm Jon Eldon," he said, forcing a smile. "I'm supposed to show you to your new quarters and answer any questions you have about life here on Xene."

The girl held out her hand and smiled broadly—a warm, friendly smile. She was not a pretty girl—rather plain, in fact. Her nose was a bit too short, her chin too round, and her face was a cloud of freckles. On top of everything else she had a mop of very red hair. She did, however, look sturdy enough. Her handclasp was firm and strong.

"I'm Beth—Beth Marden. And I'm mighty glad to be here—finally."

"Was it a good voyage?"

The girl glanced around at the milling crowd and then her gaze went out to the distant gray hills of Xene.

"Yes, they tell me it was a good trip. But six months is a long time to be cooped up. It's good to be on land again. And to be able to breathe real air again."

She took a deep breath. A look of dismay pushed away the happy expression she had had a moment earlier. She gasped and coughed in a sudden struggle for more air.

Quickly Jon unfastened his breather bottle and held the mask over her face.

"Didn't they tell you that air is thinner here on Xene than on Earth?" Jon asked angrily. Just like a girl, he thought. He knew that all new arrivals were carefully briefed on how and when to use their breathing aids. The air on Xene was breathable but there was not enough oxygen content to meet human needs. All life on Xene revolved around this one factor.

"Come," he said a little brusquely. "I'll take you to your commune building. You'll like the air there. It's treated with oxygen."

"I'm sorry I forgot about the breather bottle," Beth murmured as she walked along next to Jon.

Girls! Jon thought to himself.

At the commune building, he led Beth into the women's section and showed her the tiny cubicle that had been assigned to her. It was very small. But it contained all the things she would need in her new life. It was exactly what every other individual had—no more, no less.

A few minutes later, the two entered the noisy, crowded dining room where a special feast was being offered in honor of the new arrivals. New friendships were being formed. The boys and girls who had been on the planet for some time were gabbling away, trying to impress the newcomers with their work on the exciting Xene experiment. And the new arrivals were hurling questions at their new friends faster than they could be answered.

After they had eaten, Jon took Beth for a quick tour of the commune building—the men's section, the kitchen, the laundry, the library, and the recreation areas.

"There are five more commune buildings just like this one," Jon told his companion. She seemed eager to learn all she could.

Peering out of the corner of his eye at the excited, freckle-faced girl next to him, he felt the urge to play himself up big before her. After all, he had been here almost half a year. Only a few adults had been on Xene longer.

He led her to a quiet corner in the library and motioned for her to sit on a lounge. He sat next to her, his arm on the back of the seat.

"Well, Beth, what do you think of it?"

"It's wonderfully exciting. And it's so different than I had imagined it would be."

"Disappointed?"

"No. Just a little bewildered, I guess."

Jon smiled. "Wait until you see the mines. Then you'll really be bewildered. In fact that's why I brought you here where it is quiet. I think it only fair that you know what you're up against. It isn't easy."

"Yes, I think I have an idea." Beth grinned sheepishly. "I was a volunteer like all the others. I was told Xene is not exactly a Garden of Eden."

Jon broke out in a burst of laughter. "Anything but that. I'll take you around tomorrow. Then you'll see what you've got yourself into."

He paused. "How old are you, Beth?"

"Just sixteen."

"How long did you sign up for?"

"Two years—the same as the rest."

"That means you'll be eighteen when you leave. If you last that long."

"What do you mean?"

"I mean just that. Why do you suppose almost all the adults who came here originally have been sent back? They can't take it."

Beth stared at him.

"You'll find out sooner or later, Beth," Jon stated. "We youngsters can breathe the air on Xene if we take an extra whiff of pure oxygen every six or seven minutes. Older people have to have it every minute or so to keep going. Worse than that, they found that older people were beginning to suffer serious side effects. If they neglected to use their oxygen bottles often enough, they nearly strangled. If we go a little too long, there's not too much harm. Anyway, Beth, it does prove one thing."

"What's that?" Beth asked, her eyes shining with curiosity.

Jon almost puffed out his chest as he replied. "Xene," he said, "is one place in the universe where teen-agers like us are in control. Think of it, Beth—it may not be a Garden of Eden, but they need us here. And it belongs to boys and girls of our age. It's ours, Beth. Ours!"

* * *

Freed for a few days from his normal duties at the mine, Jon's task for the next day was to show Beth around.

They visited the other five communes. As John had told her, they were identical to the one in which she had her own quarters. Then he took her to the mine entrance a quarter mile beyond the last commune building.

Every few minutes he reminded Beth to take a deep breath from her breather bottle. After a time she did it more or less automatically.

At the mine entrance he hesitated and peered curiously at her. He thought again of the strange tunnel entrance he had found only a few days before in one of his wanderings in the hills of Xene. Would he dare take her there? Would she be frightened? Was it fair to ask her to share such a risky adventure?

He checked their breather bottles. Both were nearly full of compressed oxygen. Both, too, had their electric torches and enough water in flasks and concentrated food for the day. If only she were a boy!

"Beth," he said finally, "tomorrow is soon enough for you to visit the mine. I can tell you now—everything is clean and automatic. Not too exciting after you've worked there a few months. Would you be game to go exploring with me today?"

"Sounds exciting," she said. "After six months on the Aleron, I'm glad to be able to stretch my legs. What kind of exploring do you do here?"

"Follow along," he grinned as he grabbed her elbow and turned her away from the mine entrance. Perhaps having a girl along wasn't so bad after all.

"As you know," he said as they strode at a steady pace, taking regular sniffs from their breather bottles, "we are here to mine uranium ore which Earth needs so desperately. Oddly enough there are lots of other metals, too. Even gold. But who wants gold now? To think that a hundred years ago it was the most valued metal."

"Where do you do your exploring, Jon?" she asked, after peering around at Xene's rather dismal surface that stretched so forbiddingly in all directions.

He pointed to a stony cliff two or three miles ahead. "Up there," he said. "A few days ago I found what I think is an opening into the big mountain there behind the cliff. I didn't have a chance to explore it then."

The way was strewn with huge boulders. The climbing became a matter of clambering over and around stony obstacles. Both of them had to resort to their breather bottles at more frequent intervals.

"On Earth," Jon said as he sat down to catch his breath, "this would be like trying to walk at an elevation of 20,000 to 25,000 feet, or between four and five miles high. How do you feel?"

"A little light-headed is all. We exercised on the ship every day so I'm not too badly out of condition."

Jon looked at her with new respect. Then he

pointed at a big round boulder next to him. "This, believe it or not, is the opening."

"That boulder, an opening?"

"I don't blame you for smiling, Beth. But if you'll look closer, you'll see the boulder is different from any others around here. That made me curious. And another thing—it seems to fit very exactly into a hole in the side of the cliff—too exactly to have been done by nature."

Beth got up and took a closer look.

Jon came over and stood next to her. "I found," he said, "that it can be rolled away. There is an opening behind it. Not only that, I felt a flow of air coming out."

He looked at the girl beside him.

"Still feel like you want to try it? I'll take you back if you don't want to go in."

Beth shook her head vigorously. "I certainly don't want to go back now. Haven't you been in?"

"No, Beth. The day I found it, my breather bottle was nearly empty. I didn't dare risk it then. Today we both have nearly full bottles. What do you say, Beth? Game to try it with me?"

"Could it be some animal's lair?"

"I don't think so. There are no surface animals on Xene that we have been able to find. In the mines they have found evidence of some reptile-like creatures. I have never seen any. And anyway, I have my blaster with me."

He paused.

"Let's sit down for a few minutes. Before we go

in, I think I should tell you about this planet. Maybe you've heard it all before. More likely you haven't."

He pointed off toward the cluster of domed commune buildings which could be seen in the distance.

"All those people—over a thousand of us—are engaged in taking uranium ore out of one comparatively small area of perhaps two or three square miles. We don't even have to dig tunnels. They are already there. In fact, the geologists who surveyed the region originally said the whole area as far as we can see in all directions contains a maze of tunnels. Probably tens of thousands of miles of them, they say."

"And you think this opening leads into the tunnels in this area?"

"I'd sure like to find out."

Again, Jon felt the urge to impress Beth. "The people who lived on this planet became extinct, it is believed, not so many years ago. But while they lived, they must have spent their whole time burrowing through the underlying rock like moles."

"But why?"

"That's the question I've been asking myself. Why? Why should they cut tunnels, mile after mile? The scientists who came here last year to study the question have all been sent back to Earth. They were unable to stand up under the air problem. That's why I'd like to do some exploring of my own."

"I don't understand, Jon. What were they after,

those original natives? Why did they do it? What kind of people were they?"

Jon shrugged his shoulders. "It would seem to me they were after something more precious to them than metals. Ancient ruins of their cities have been found, but they were abandoned thousands of years ago. In taking out the uranium ore from our mines, we have found evidence that a few remaining survivors were living there possibly as recently as five or ten years ago."

"Do you think there might be any left in this area?"

"It's possible. But not likely. The planet has no surface water. It once did. Xene was probably very much like Earth at one time. It's amazing the race survived as long as it did without better conditions for growing food."

Beth jumped to her feet. She took a big whiff of oxygen from her breather bottle and faced Jon. Her eyes shone with eager anticipation.

"It's thrilling. I wonder what we'll find behind that boulder?"

"Are you sure you want to risk it?"

"I wouldn't miss this for anything. Why, we might be making history. It's for adventure like this that I volunteered to come to Xene."

"It could be dangerous."

"Now who's holding back?" Beth laughed as she put her hand on the boulder and tried to push it aside.

Jon then put his shoulder to the heavy stone.

Slowly it rolled away from the opening. A flow of air came up to meet them.

Electric torch in hand, Jon peered warily into the dark passageway. Then, lowering his body in feet first, he slid within. Beth quickly followed. With both pulling they were able to roll the boulder back into its snug place.

Jon's torch showed a carefully cut tunnel that led downward at a slight slant as far as the beam could reach.

"Still game?" Jon asked.

"Lead on, Marco Polo. We've a new world to discover."

After a few hundred feet, the tunnel branched out into three different directions. So far there had been no obstacles in the passageway, nothing to hinder their moving easily.

Suddenly Jon stopped and grabbed Beth's arm.

"We've forgotten something! We've forgotten to use our breather bottles. I haven't used mine since we came into the tunnel."

He took a deep breath of the tunnel air.

"That's strange," he said. "The air here is better than it is outside. Much better. Perhaps we can get along without our breather bottles here."

"Isn't that true in the mines?" Beth asked.

"No. We use our breather bottles all day while we work there, the same as outside. This is a real discovery."

"That should make it easier for us, shouldn't it?"

"Yes, it should," Jon stated. "But right now we have a problem for ourselves. We have three passageways to choose from. We can't risk getting lost. For all I know, these tunnels go for miles. We ought to have some way to mark our route so we can find our way back. I'd sure hate to be buried alive in here."

Beth shivered at the thought and intuitively came closer to him as though for protection.

"So far we aren't in any trouble. We'll take the passage to the right. If only we had something to mark where we go."

"I have a lipstick," Beth said as she dug into the pocket of her jump suit and pulled it out. "Having a girl along is good for that much anyway."

"Good!" Jon cried as he took the lipstick and unscrewed the top. He then put a mark on the edge of the tunnel they had just left.

They moved on. At intervals they began to find side tunnels which merely led into rooms carved out of the rock.

Some of the rooms were completely empty. Others contained miscellaneous debris. All looked as if they may have been lived in at one time. In one room Jon saw what he thought was a mound of skeletons, piled almost to the ceiling. He quickly backed out and half pushed Beth past the entrance. Frequently they stumbled over rock that had fallen.

They plunged on, eager to see what the next passageway would reveal to them. It was an adventure such as neither had ever experienced before.

Half stumbling, half crawling, they crossed one especially stone-littered place when Jon put his hand out to stop Beth.

"Listen!" he said. Beth paused.

"It's falling water," Beth whispered. "I can hear it. And that reminds me that I'm thirsty."

Slowly they made their way across another pile of fallen rock. There, at their feet, lay a miniature underground lake.

Jon played his torch across the surface. The light was reflected back by the blackness of the water. Somewhere off in the distance they could hear the splash of water coming into the lake from a small stream.

"We'd better save our own flasks of water for later. There isn't much water in Xene. Here, hold the torch," he said. "I'll taste the water here."

So far Beth had not used her own torch to conserve its power. She took Jon's and directed the beam down at the water while he lowered himself to his knees to scoop up a cupped handful.

With his hands a scant inch from the water's surface, he paused. He stared down into the black water. With horror he saw, just below the surface, glaring up at him the face of a huge fish—a malevolent face, a face of evil, with twin rows of needle-like teeth.

Slowly he stood up. He took the torch from Beth's hands and brought it down close to the water's surface. The fish had disappeared.

"What is it?" Beth cried.

"There's some kind of life down there in the water. A fish probably. But very big. All I really saw was that it had two rows of sharp teeth and it looked very deadly."

"I didn't see anything."

"I'm glad you didn't," Jon said. "Look, Beth, I still think we should take a drink here. If fish live in it, it must be safe. I have a bandage in my first aid kit. I'll let it soak up the water and we can squeeze it into our mouths. I don't like the idea of putting my hand in there."

After five minutes or so of laboriously dunking the cloth and squeezing out the water, they were just about satisfied.

"One more time," Jon said. He dipped the cloth into the water. There was a sudden swirl and the cloth was torn from his hand, shredded in half by the sharp teeth of the creature.

Beth uttered a sharp cry as she staggered back, almost dropping the torch. Jon, in turning to save her from falling, stumbled and fell sideways toward the lake's edge. Frantically he clutched at the tiny stone ridges to keep from sliding across the slimy rock into the water. With a strenuous twist of his body he held on.

"Whew! That was close," he muttered as he scrambled to his feet. "Let's get out of here."

Almost headlong they ran along the lake's edge to another passageway.

"Jon," Beth said, as they halted to catch their

breath, "did you mark that last tunnel we came out of?"

"Yes, of course. I haven't missed yet. You don't think I'd forget that, do you?"

Jon felt a bit miffed at his headlong flight. He felt his pride had been hurt.

"No, Jon. I just don't remember your doing it."

"OK, Beth. I think it's time we turned back anyway. I'll prove to you I've marked every passageway we've come through."

At the first multi-crossing, he looked all around for the lipstick marking.

"This is the place I thought you'd missed," Beth said weakly.

"Just help me look. I know it's here somewhere."

For several minutes they looked for the mark. Finally Jon said, "Well, it really doesn't matter. I remember it well. We came out here and there was a tunnel on each side of us and one in front. We took the one in front. All we have to do is take the middle one and in a few minutes we'll be back at the lake. From there I know we've made marks all the way out."

For ten minutes they trudged through the passageway, going past debris-filled rooms and climbing over fallen rocks.

"It wasn't this far to the lake," Beth said.

Jon stopped. "I'm sorry Beth, but I think you are right. And if you are right, we're really lost."

* * *

For several hours they stumbled on, often feeling their way in the dark to conserve the power of their electric torches.

Jon felt crushed. He had acted the fool. Now, somehow, he had to lead them out of the maze.

How big was it? A few acres or a few hundred square miles?

From the way both of them had been faltering, Jon was ready to admit they had better conserve not only their light but their strength.

"Let's stop here and rest," he said half-heartedly. All he heard by way of reply from Beth was a sigh of relief and a faint sound as she slid down to the floor.

Jon could tell by her regular breathing that she was asleep almost instantly. For several minutes he sat with his back to the tunnel wall, his extinguished torch in one hand and his blaster in the other. He listened with all his might, but all he heard was the terrible, dead silence of the place.

He awoke with a start. Something had awakened him. Beth was still sleeping, her breathing coming in little gaspy sounds.

He felt with his hands for the torch and blaster that he had dropped between his knees. Slowly he raised them, one in each hand.

He flashed on the torch and directed the beam down the tunnel the way they had come.

There—filling the passageway—was a huge, reptilian, crocodile-type creature fully fifteen feet long. Its four-foot jaws were open revealing four rows of long, pointed teeth. One more twist of its body and it would have reached the sleeping girl.

At that instant Jon fired his blaster.

Beth awoke and screamed.

Jon, shaken, climbed awkwardly to his feet and seized Beth's outstretched hand. He pulled her away from the animal where it lay, twisting and turning on the floor only a few feet from them.

"Let's get out of here," Beth cried as she watched in horror the writhing death throes of the beast.

What next? Jon wondered as he hurried Beth away from the thrashing sounds of the dying animal.

Blindly they plunged on. After several minutes they paused to catch their breath and calm their shattered nerves.

As they sat there, something began to disturb Jon. It was a subtle nudge to his senses. He tried to figure out what it was. Then he realized it was a faint vibration in the floor on which they sat.

"Do you feel it too?" he asked Beth.

"Feel what? Right now I'm too scared and too numb to feel anything."

"Listen. Don't you feel a kind of vibration?"

For several minutes they sat in silence.

"Yes, Jon, I agree. I do feel something."

"Let's go on. If there is a vibration, it may be our miners at work."

They got to their feet and moved slowly on. When they reached crossings, they tried to feel which tunnel held the most vibration.

Gradually the sound turned into a whirring, grinding noise.

"I may be mistaken," Jon said, "but it sounds like machinery."

The sound grew louder and louder. Finally they could sense that whatever was making the noise was just ahead—around the next turn.

They hurried forward.

Bursting out of the tunnel's end, they found themselves in a huge cavern. It was fully two hundred feet long, almost as wide, and over a hundred feet high.

Far overhead they could see a waterfall turning a water wheel. The whirring sound they had heard from the distance was now a crushing, crunching roar. The vibration was the mechanism of the ancient water-driven machinery badly in need of oil.

"It's a power plant," Jon cried out. "It's an old-fashioned power plant using the power of falling water. The old inhabitants of the planet must have built it and it's been running ever since."

"But why?" Beth asked. "What did they use the power for? I see no electric wires, no lights, no heating arrangements. What did it drive?"

Jon looked around, directing the beam of his electric torch in all directions. He walked over to a pile of crushed rock that lay in a pile on the floor.

"Very strange," he said, as he fingered the stuff. He shook his head in wonder.

"Did you ever take chemistry?" he asked Beth.

"One short course is all."

"I had two years of it. I'm just now beginning to get a faint idea what this is all about."

"It's all a great mystery to me, Jon."

"Well, I'm not sure I'm on the right track. But if what I think is here, it begins to make sense. And it gives me more respect for the ancients who lived here."

"I'm glad to hear that something is beginning to make sense to you. Everything so far has me very confused."

"Listen, Beth. What would have been more precious to the ancients than uranium or gold or any other metal? The answer is right there for us to see. It was air! At least oxygen!"

Jon turned his torch beam upward toward the turning of the water wheel.

"I remember our chemistry instructor telling us there were several ways to make oxygen artificially. One of the ways had to do with heating and mixing a combination of manganese dioxide with some kind of chlorate. Potassium chlorate, I think it was. I'm even surprised I remember it. I recall he told us something else that amazed us all—that rock is fifty percent oxygen."

He paused.

"Don't you see, Beth? It could be possible that air on the surface became too thin for the ancients. Someone may have developed some kind of process to extract oxygen out of rock. Then they went underground. It would explain their passion for digging."

"But why the water wheel power plant?"

"As I said, there are several ways to make oxygen artificially, at least to extract it from whatever is holding it. One explanation for the water wheel is they used the power to crush the rock for processing. Or they might have used it to make a primitive electric generating plant. If they did this, they could use the direct current to pass through water. In this way water is decomposed, or as they say, electrolyzed, and the oxygen content can be collected. This usually takes more electrical power than I think this water wheel can produce. Maybe not. Maybe when it was new and operating smoothly it could do the job. Anyway we know that the tunnels have more oxygen content than the air outside. Something created it."

"Are those the ways they make oxygen on Earth?" Beth asked, somewhat befuddled by the explanation.

"No," Jon replied. "But I don't believe this water power plant has sufficient capacity to produce the power to compress the outside air into a liquid. If they could have done that, they would simply let the liquid air stand. When the nitrogen boiled away, what was left would be pure liquid oxygen. It's not an easy process. I can't believe those ancient people had the skill to do it."

"What killed them?" Beth asked.

"Who knows? After leaving their cities on the surface, it may have taken thousands of years for them to die out. Somewhere along the line, the odds became too great for them. They probably had terrible health problems trying to live underground. And food must have been a major need. It's quite obvious, though, that in the end the race died. We may never know exactly why."

Beth sighed wearily. "There is one thing I'd like to know. When are *we* going to get out of here? And how?"

After a few hours of fitful rest, disturbed by the screeching and squealing of the ancient water wheel, Jon decided he had better make a thorough search of the cavern.

There were several passageways leading away from the room. All looked alike.

He peered at the waterfall far overhead. If it had not been so high, he would have considered trying to follow it to its source. There was no possible way up to it that he could see.

Even though everything in the place was crude and primitive, Jon had to marvel at the labor and ingenuity that had gone into the making of the whole arrangement.

The more he looked, the more he was convinced that its sole purpose was to manufacture oxygen. The mere fact that it was still operating, however poorly, and the tunnels were richer in oxygen than the air on the outside, seemed proof enough.

What a story he would be able to tell the people back at the communes. Unbelievable as it was, they would have to believe when he showed them the ancient power plant, still running. What a tale to tell!

But then reality rushed back on him. Unless they found a way out, they were trapped. And as far as he could see there was no sure way out. He wouldn't be able to tell about their discoveries unless he could find a way out of the maze.

Beth touched his arm. "We aren't going to make it, are we, Jon?"

"Of course we are. We've got to."

"Have you any kind of plan?"

"Not yet. But I'll think of something."

"We just can't stay here," Beth murmured as she scraped her foot across the dusty floor of the cavern. "A thousand years of dirt," she said.

Jon was looking down at her foot. "Do that again, Beth."

"Do what?"

"Move your foot across the floor. No, wait, I'll help."

Beth watched in wonder as Jon scraped his feet across the floor, pushing away the dust of years. When he had a space cleared, he peered down at it.

"Just a lot of lines cut into the floor," Beth said without interest. "We should be starting. Let's go."

"No. Just a minute."

Gradually Jon cleared away a space twenty feet by twenty feet. The lines on the floor ended in a perimeter line. Only two or three lines went on beyond the perimeter line.

"You know what I think this is, Beth?"

"Just a lot of lines cut into the floor."

"You're right, Beth. But if they represent what I think they represent, they may tell us how to get out of here. To me, this looks like a map of the tunnels in this area. It makes sense that they would have some way to keep track of where they were going."

"A map, Jon? A real map?"

"Well, look here. In the center is a square. It could represent this big cavern. Then off in that direction where there is a line, there is a tunnel exit. And one over there. And still another over there. All the exits from the cavern are located exactly as they are marked on this floor map."

"But can you find out which tunnel to take?"

"I'm going to try. All I have to do is study the lines in this map and then take the one that goes all the way to the perimeter. There we'll take one of those outer lines to the surface. I'm going to copy out the route on a sheet of paper I have in my pocket."

"Do you think it will work?"

"It's got to work. Our electric torches are good for only a few more hours."

For several minutes Jon puzzled over the grooves cut in the stone floor. Then he quickly sketched out the course that looked most promising. He marked approximate distances, turns, and cross passageways.

Finally, smiling hopefully, he helped the weary Beth to her feet.

From the cavern exit he took a last look at the

noisily clanking water wheel. Then he concentrated on following the twists and turns indicated on his copied map.

Several times he had to stop and carefully estimate which tunnel to take. Mostly he felt he was hitting each cross tunnel right on the mark.

It took them less than two hours to reach the opening to the outside. It was a different place from where they had entered. The exit hole, however, was protected by a similar boulder arrangement.

After pulling Beth out of the narrow opening, he carefully rolled the boulder back into place.

They paused to look out over the scene below them. It was night. The only light came from two of Xene's four moons. Off in the distance they could see the faint light that marked the commune buildings.

Beth heaved a big sigh of relief. "I must admit, Jon, that you have given me a very exciting first day on Xene."

Jon held her by the arm as they started to make their way slowly down the cliffside.

"It was exciting for me, too. And now, Beth, we'd better go back to using our breather bottles. No use taking any more chances."

Best Friend

A. M. LIGHTNER

DR. Hercules Valla, eminent scientist, made the final adjustments to the electrodes and let his hand linger affectionately upon Candy's woolly head.

"Good dog," he said softly, mindful of the fact that some of the other people working in the shed might think it odd to hear a man of his standing talking to his experimental animal.

Candy's tongue licked Dr. Valla's hand. She lay relaxed upon her foam rubber shock absorber and watched him with loving, trustful eyes.

"Everything's going to be fine," he muttered, scratching her ears and smoothing down her tail under the harness. "In a few hours you'll be back with us, and this time it's for keeps. You're being retired to house pet, Candy. We'll get you a husband and you can have your pups on my bed."

Candy licked him again and Valla hastily withdrew his hand and snapped the plastic dome into place, while sternly repressing the feelings of reluctance and dread that invariably assailed him at this point.

"She's all yours," he said to the waiting mechanics, and walked off without stopping to watch them fit the capsule into the waiting nose cone.

Outside he met his friend, the mathematician, Dr. Milton Rowan. The younger man fell into step beside him.

"Got Candy all trussed up?" he asked. "Said a fond farewell? You want to watch that talking to your animals! Next thing to talking to yourself."

"She needs a morale booster like anyone else. I'd like to see you take off on this joy ride without even a kiss from your wife."

"If I intended to ride a rocket, I'd keep my wife as far away as possible. Glad I didn't go into that end of the business! Don't you think it's a little underhanded to tell the poor pooch that everything's going to be fine, when you know any of a dozen disasters is possible?"

Dr. Valla shuddered. "It isn't reassurance she needs. It's love and my approval. You can't train an animal without that. And I wouldn't be doing this work if I didn't know there's going to be a man riding that thing soon."

"Yes, they've got the bugs pretty well ironed out," said Rowan. "I don't think you need worry about Candy—much. Where are you planning to watch it?"

"The boat's leaving any minute. Got to get down

range where they expect to pick her up." He stopped to fumble in his pockets and withdrew a small, oblong box. "Candy wouldn't forgive me if I turned up without these."

Dr. Rowan squinted at the yellow package labeled "Canine Yum-Yums."

"You'll never learn not to get emotionally involved with your experiment! Well, I've got to get back to my computers. I'll see you when it's over."

The countdown proceeded without a hitch. The launching was successful, and as the vehicle roared skyward, Dr. Rowan found himself muttering "Lucky dog!" and then smiling as he thought of his friend, speeding across the ocean toward a rendezvous at a time and place calculated by his machines.

"Good thing she didn't blow," he said to a watching scientist. "I believe it'd break Valla's heart if anything happened to that dog now. It's the third time she's been up and she's due for retirement. Funny how some men let themselves get involved with their tools of trade."

"Don't kid yourself," said the other. "How'd you feel if someone or something smashed up that computer of yours?"

The very thought made Rowan stutter. "Why, I . . . I . . . that would be criminal! And besides it isn't a risk of the experiment."

"At least you could rebuild the computer," said the man.

At this point the work of that instrument claimed Dr. Rowan's attention and he had no time to think of a fitting reply. The signals from the rocket had to be fed into the machine, together with the reports of sightings as they came in. The orbit had to be figured and the points of re-entry and landing sent to the distant ship. Dr. Rowan was absorbed with details and only later did an ugly fact begin to dawn upon him. The rocket was not in the proper orbit.

"Tell them to hurry up and eject that capsule," he ordered, "or it's going to be too late."

He continued to work with the computer, and not till well along in the morning was he finally convinced of his results. Then he sat back to relax and glanced up at the military man leaning over his shoulder.

"Well, did you eject?" he snapped.

The man shook his head. "The mechanism failed to work. And it seems to be too far away now. When do you figure it'll be back again?"

Rowan experienced a sinking sensation. "That thing isn't coming back," he said. "Not for a long time. It's headed out beyond Jupiter."

He threw down his pencil in annoyance. Why should he feel this way? It was only a dog—not a man. But he kept seeing Hercules Valla, standing on a pitching deck with a box of Canine Yum-Yums in his hand.

The satellite raced on into outer space. Candy lay in her little nest and drowsed. For that is what dogs do when waiting for their master. The unpleasant acceleration, which she had learned to expect at the beginning of a flight, was over. She was not unduly troubled by the feeling of weightlessness, for she was held by the straps of her harness. The electrodes sent back to earth the record of her breathing and her heartbeat until the distance became too great for the tiny radio to span. Candy slept, her ears ever alert for the click of the capsule's opening to tell her that her master was there.

In the far reaches of the solar system the satellite was a meteor, hurtling along with its own thrust, its orbit determined by the pull of the celestial bodies that it passed. But space is infinite compared with earth. The billions of suns and their attendant planets harbor many wonders. And on a little moon of an outer planet, two such wonders were sitting when Candy's vehicle shot past.

Kondar and Zylph had been scouting the galaxy and paused to rest and set up their instruments on this convenient island in space. They knew that habitable planets are few and far between, and the chance of finding one with intelligent life even less likely. But intelligent life at the same point of development as their race—beings who could talk sensibly, act cooperatively and generally communicate on the same level of understanding—that had never been found in the ten thousand years that their people had been at large in the galaxy.

Kondar was adjusting an instrument much like the telescope, while Zylph busied himself with setting up a temporary dwelling. Kondar called to his friend.

"There's something interesting here. Come and

take a look. Too big to be a meteor. Too small to be a moon of any sort. And besides it looks peculiar."

Zylph obliged by squinting through the instrument.

"Definitely not natural," he declared. "Hurry up and catch it before it gets away."

Since their spaceship was far, far in advance of anything dreamed of on earth, it took Kondar only a short time to catch up with the satellite and bring it back to the little moon. Zylph had the temporary headquarters ready. The nose cone was set down; the lid was pried off; and the two galactic beings stared at Candy and her trappings.

"It's unbelievable!" cried Kondar. "Intelligent life in this unlikely spot!"

"It looks rather dead," said Zylph. "And it's all strapped up. It couldn't be piloting the vessel in that condition."

"Not intelligent," guessed Kondar. "No hands, you see. Probably a lower form sent as an experiment. You realize what this means, Zylph! There must be intelligent beings back where this came from, and they're just beginning to learn about space flight."

"And we discovered them!" sighed Zylph. "On our first hundredth trip!"

"Well, let's examine it! Get the revitalizer and the translator. Get the thought analyzer. We mustn't miss our big chance!"

So Candy was revitalized. She was taken out of her cocoon and fed and watered and treated with the utmost care. She didn't like the smell of the strange people who let her out of her cage, but she was a tractable animal. She had learned to accept many peculiar things. She ate and drank what was offered and submitted when more machines and electrodes were fixed upon her. But all the time she was wishing that Dr. Valla would come and put an end to this foolishness. On every previous flight the door of the cage had been opened by her beloved master proffering candy, and she had no doubt that in the fullness of time he would appear.

The translator quickly demonstrated that dogs do not speak or have a language. But Kondar was not discouraged. He merely switched on the "brain analyzer." This remarkable machine could take thought pictures and emotions directly from the brain waves of the subject, and from it Kondar and Zylph received their first impression of the planet Earth.

They quickly realized that Kondar's guess had been correct. The masters of the planet, seen through the eyes of this animal, were very intelligent and remarkable creatures. Practically gods of their world.

But it was more than that. As the "analyzer" was turned up, the two aliens were suffused with a surging blast of love.

"Did you feel that?" asked Zylph in an awed whisper.

"Almost knocked me down," agreed Kondar.

"But don't you realize," chattered Zylph, his excitement rising, "any people able to inspire love like that in the lower animals must be wonderful!"

"And we know that they've reached a high technical level. They're about to burst out into the galaxy. Zylph, my friend, we've found what everyone's dreamed of since we first hit space!"

"A brother planet," breathed Zylph. "A species to share the galaxy with! Do you think we can find where this thing came from?"

"Must be one of the inner planets in this system. All we have to do is go in and look. You and I are going to be famous!"

The two aliens gathered up their gear, dismantled their shelter, and packed everything, including Candy and her capsule, into their spaceship.

By the time they reached the orbit of Jupiter it was evident that they were headed in the right direction. In spite of the electronic noise coming from the giant planet, their sensitive instruments were able to pick up radio signals that could only be made by intelligent beings. By the time they hit the orbit of Mars, it was coming in clearly and they were receiving the voices of the strangers. They hooked up their translating machine and proceeded to a landing on the third planet's moon.

So Kondar and Zylph listened to a sampling of an ordinary night's radio, and their first impulse to make quick contact with the new world was arrested. The music was an uproar to their ears. The advertising made no sense. But it was the news that overwhelmed them.

A frenzied voice told of gang warfare in the big cities, of murder in Texas and kidnapping in Iowa. It described a new "antimatter" bomb and gave an account of renewed bloodshed in Africa. It ended with a report on the peace talks in Geneva, where another snag had developed.

At this point, Kondar reached out and switched off the translator. The voice went on yammering in the same foreign tongue, but it was a relief not to be able to understand it.

"There seems to be something wrong somewhere."

Zylph nodded miserably. "Only just this side of barbarism. We were fools to think we could beat the Old Ones at this game."

"But the animal," Kondar protested. "There was no mistake about that. We both felt it. How could an animal like this—intelligent as such creatures go—feel this blind, adoring love for these . . . these . . . ?"

"I know," said Zylph sadly. "There must be something there. Something we've missed. Perhaps in ten thousand years . . ."

"When we are dust. That's always the way. We're either too early or too late. Well, we'd better clear out before one of them spots us. If they're beginning to have space travel, we don't want them to follow us home. In their present state they won't be fit to live with."

Zylph agreed, but as they prepared to take off for the second time, they were startled by the strange behavior of the animal. Candy had risen to her feet with her eyes on the instrument "speaker" where a new voice from the planet was being piped into the ship. Her ears were cocked, her tail was up. She gave voice to a soft whine that started low down and rose in intensity till it erupted in a series of quick, eager barks. Soon she was running about the cabin, searching for the voice and crying pathetically. Then she lay down as near the source of the sound as possible, while a low moan came from her throat, the essence of loneliness and despair.

Kondar switched on the translator and a different voice came over. "You have just heard Dr. Hercules Valla, speaking for better international friendship and agreement to ban atomic testing. Dr. Valla is with the space-flight program being carried on in our state and we are fortunate to have him tonight as a guest. Our next speaker will be . . ."

A third voice took over, but Candy had lost interest. Zylph switched off the receiver and they both stared at the animal. The two aliens vividly remembered those pulsing waves of love.

"What are we going to do with this creature?" Kondar voiced the thought that was troubling them both.

"It's a pity to take her away. She wouldn't be happy with us."

"You know the rules. We must leave no trace of our visit."

"But that voice was the man she loves. Can't we send her back to him?"

"Don't be foolish. How could she find him in a

whole world? And could we do it without their knowing?"

"We still have her harness and parachute. We could take her down most of the way. The voice was coming from that long spit of land. I could almost pinpoint it."

"Well, it's against all the regulations. But there never was a case quite like this. Get the harness on her while I take us down."

Hercules Valla and Milton Rowan were going home after the lecture. Dr. Rowan had insisted on driving his friend, for you could never be sure, under the circumstances, whether he had his mind on what he was doing.

It was a beautiful moonlit night and by common consent they stopped along a deserted beach to enjoy the peace and beauty of the ocean. Ever since the last shoot, Dr. Valla had been silent and withdrawn, and Rowan was worried by his friend's despondent mood. And so he was relieved when the doctor began to speak.

"Look at her up there," said Hercules Valla, pointing at the moon. "What won't Man do to get there!"

He stopped and Rowan had the uncomfortable feeling that the soft-hearted scientist was going to cry. He searched his brain frantically for something cheerful to say. Something to make the failure sound like success, to make Candy's sacrifice constructive. He was about to come out with some ill-chosen words when Valla held up a hand and Rowan realized that he was listening intently.

"Don't you hear it?" asked Dr. Valla. "There's a dog barking."

Now he's really off his rocker, thought Rowan, but he only said, "I don't hear anything."

"You've been listening to your old machine for so long that you're getting deaf." And Dr. Valla began to whistle in a high, peculiar way.

Rowan became alarmed. If this weren't his best friend, he'd certainly describe the fellow as batty. Valla surely had been overworking. He'd better get him to a doctor when he got back to the base.

And then inconceivably there was a noise in the bushes. A rushing, a scrabbling, accompanied by a high-pitched whining, and a small dog burst from the underbrush and threw itself upon Dr. Valla. In the uncertain moonlight, assisted by the glare from the headlights, Dr. Rowan saw that it did look very much like Herc's experimental animal. Its back was marked with the same dark patches, and its tail vibrated with all the frantic excitement of a one-man dog that has been separated too long from its master. Dr. Rowan wondered if he was losing his mind, too.

"Now get hold of yourself, Valla," he cautioned. "This thing's upset you so that every friendly dog you meet in the bush sets you thinking about Candy."

"But it *is* Candy!" cried Dr. Valla. "Can't you see? Can't you hear her?" He picked the dog up to let it lick his face, and went off into a string of endearments that were nauseating to Rowan.

"Now look here, Valla. The dog may look like Candy and it may sound like Candy—but it can't *be* Candy. You mustn't let yourself be carried away by these fantasies. I've been warning you to keep a hold on reality."

"Oh, is that so!" said Dr. Valla sharply. "I guess I should know my own animal."

Rowan could see that this was going to be quite a problem, and he cursed himself for having agreed to stop and look at the moon.

"Be reasonable," he argued. "If that's Candy, how did she get here? You know we plotted her orbit out beyond Jupiter."

"That's easy," said Dr. Valla. "Your plottings were wrong. The capsule made a smaller orbit and came around and landed somewhere near here, where it wasn't expected."

"But that's quite impossible! It was picked up by all the tracking stations. In fact, we had radio contact for a good part of the distance. And it was all worked out and verified by my computer."

"All I can say is that your computer was wrong."

Rowan sputtered at the insult. "Wrong! My computer wrong! Do you realize what you're saying?"

"Yes, wrong. Blew a fuse, split a gasket, or whatever it is computers do."

"But that's impossible. If anything goes wrong, it gives a signal. And nothing has gone wrong. It's worked perfectly since then. It figured the orbits for the next shoot."

"Well, you'd better refigure them then. There's liable to be all kinds of errors."

Rowan shuddered at the mere possibility. He drew himself up to reply.

"My computer," he said, "has never been wrong. I might be wrong—but not the computer. And you'd better get hold of yourself, man. How will this sound to the scientists at the base? Too much brooding over a lost pet. All too easy to mistake the first friendly stray."

Dr. Valla stopped scratching Candy's ears. "If I were on a desert island," he said, "or the surface of the moon, and you appeared unexpectedly, covered with dirt and unshaven, I would still know it was you. Because I know you. You're my friend. I could never mistake you no matter how peculiar or inexplicable the circumstances. And I could not mistake Candy. This is Candy."

The dog pricked up her ears at the name and whined ecstatically. Valla carried her to the car lights.

"Look here, if you have to have proof. Look at the marks of the harness. She must have squeezed out of it somehow. And here, feel under her coat. A part of the harness is still there!"

Against his will, Dr. Rowan felt. As he brushed the fur, the dog gave a low growl and her head whipped around with bared fangs. Rowan jerked back, but not before his fingers knew the truth of Valla's statement.

The professor laughed. "She never did like you, did she? Must sense that you prefer your machines."

Dr. Rowan remembered other occasions when Candy had snapped at him, and his mind tottered on the abyss.

"If it's true, where's the capsule?"

"I don't suppose we'll ever find that. But if we search the neighborhood in the morning, we ought to find the parachute."

Dr. Rowan did not answer. His mind was hastily turning over all the possibilities about the faulty computer. What could be the matter with it? Something terrible. Irreparable. He felt his life's work crumbling, and made his way blindly to the car.

"Where are you going?" asked Dr. Valla.

"Got to get back and look at my computer. Got to figure this out."

"Good idea," said Valla. "But don't let it get you down. We have to keep a good hold on reality these days."

Rowan's reply was to rev the motor, so Valla climbed in beside him and held the door open.

"Hop in, Candy," he said. "We're going home."

Venusian Invader

LARRY STERNIG

MART Wells shut off the alarm buzzer and jumped out of bed—much to his regret. He cussed and then grinned sheepishly as he was brought up with a thud against the fortunately unbreakable glass of the window. A year on Callisto, and he could still forget that he weighed only thirty-six pounds and couldn't take a normal step without neutronium-weighted shoes.

Regaining his balance, he yawned and looked out over the rough Callisto landscape beyond Comprotown. Then he yawned again and reached for his uniform.

A year before, Comprotown—and his job as rocketport dispatcher—had been Romance with a capital R. Now, he thought gloomily, Romance with Leah with a capital L. and a lot of good that did him when Leah Barrow's father was Old Fish-face himself, Director of Comprotown.

True, Comprotown held fewer than a thousand colonists, but it was the only inhabited spot on bleak Callisto, and its Director was practically czar of a world. Yes, the Director could well afford to look down his long nose at any uniform with fewer than six stars on its right sleeve. But Leah didn't feel that—

Suddenly, straightening up as he fastened his weighted boot, he looked more intently out of the window. Something that flashed caught his eye out in the barren, warped hills. A gleam of metal where metal shouldn't have been. And it looked like a small spaceship.

Mart hastily pulled on his other boot and ran down the stairs. A redheaded mechanic from the rocketport was coming out of the building across the way.

Mart called out, "Red! Something about a mile back in the hills looks like a spaceship. Has one been reported down?"

"Huh?" The mechanic looked startled. "You sure? No, there hasn't been a report. Wait, I'll radio Central Communications."

He darted back into the building, and emerged a moment later. "No report. They're going to send out the autogiro to look at it. Say, Mart, there are only two small spaceships on Callisto. Could it be—"

Mart was already running toward the corner from which he could see the landing field. He stopped so suddenly that the mechanic almost ran into him, and said, "Whew! They're both there." Leah Barrow's trim little spacecruiser was safe in port. So was the Police one-seater scout—but that wasn't the one Mart had looked for first.

From near the Administration Building a two-place autogiro was rising, silhouetted for a moment between the horns of the reddish crescent of big Jupiter just above the horizon.

As he walked across the field toward headquarters, Mart surveyed the familiar scene. Three squat freighters were up on the racks, their ugly black bottoms over the ash-filled blasting pits; four others were on dollies ready to be serviced.

All seven were ready for their regular weekly Callisto-Jupe hop, ready to pick up more ore. And, as usual, they'd go out today to clear the field for the sleeker, faster, long-haul ships that would arrive from Earth tomorrow for the smelted metal. Mart glanced at his wrist-chronometer. Eight o'clock now; in an hour and a half, *Freighter One,* right on schedule, would start testing its rocket tubes for the ten o'clock hop. And an hour later, *Freighter Two* would start to warm up for the eleven o'clock blasting-off. And then the others, every hour on the hour.

At his desk in the Administration Building, Mart picked up the familiar sheaf of clearance papers waiting for his attention, and glanced through them. Initialing them was mere routine; they'd never cleared a minute early or a minute late since he'd been there. Director Barrow saw to that.

The door opened. Mart put down the papers and glanced up.

One of the workmen from the smelting plant, a tall black-haired fellow wearing tinted glasses, stood looking into the office. Mart didn't remember ever seeing him before—but with several hundred workmen, you couldn't remember all of them.

"Director Barrow in?"

Mart glanced up at the wall clock before he answered. "He'll be here in twenty-one minutes. Sit down and wait if you're off duty."

He turned back to the papers and finished initialing them, grinning inwardly at being able to say that the Director would arrive in twenty-one minutes exactly. It wasn't everywhere that one could make so accurate a prediction about anyone's arrival time, but Barrow was something of a chronometer himself.

He tossed the papers toward the back of the desk and threw the switch of the communicator on his desk, leaned forward slightly. "Dispatcher Wells calling Police Autogiro."

"Autogiro, Captain Wayne," came the reply. "Go ahead, Mart."

"I was the one who reported seeing the spaceship, Cap—if it was one. Found it? If not, I can—"

"Thanks, Mart, but we've sighted it all right. We're now circling, looking for a spot to come down. It doesn't take much, but damned if we can perch on a ridge like a canary. Neither could that space-speedster down there.

"Wrecked? What's it look like?"

"Ummm. Offhand one of the single-place jobs that Venusians bought from Earth before the war. Full armament, too."

"What? You sure, Cap? After the Earth-Venus twenty-two eighty treaty, we reclaimed and destroyed all the armed—"

"Yeah, I know," cut in the Captain's voice. "All but a few that the Venusian renegades—the pirates—got off with before then. Well—we're going down. Corey's found a place not too far from it where he can set the giro down, or says he can."

"If that's a pirate ship, Cap, be careful!"

"Don't worry. We're armed. And the ship's pretty smashed up. Probably at least kayoed whoever was in it. Well, keep your key open and I'll call you back. We're down."

Mart found the shipment chart and began to check off tonnage. That much he wanted to get out of the way before—but something was gnawing at the back of his mind. It took him a moment to trace what it was. Of course. The workman who was waiting for the Director was wearing tinted glasses.

Tinted glasses on Callisto! It didn't make sense. The sun, half a billion miles away, gives only a twenty-fifth of the light that falls on Earth. Even when that light is augmented by Big Jupe, it isn't— Yes, it was the first time he'd seen tinted glasses in Comprotown.

Curiously, he turned to glance at the seated workman. But the carrier wave of the desk communicator hummed and he forgot his visitor as Captain Wayne's voice boomed in.

"Dispatcher Wells. Captain Wayne calling Dispatcher—"

"Okay, Cap. Go ahead."

"We've examined the spaceship. No one's in it, hurt or otherwise. It's a single seater. A pirate ship all right."

"You sure? How can you be certain?"

"Aside from the fact that it would have no business around here if it wasn't, the papers are a giveaway. There's a whole sheaf of them. Reports on the Ganymede jewel shipments mostly. And a full set of data on our own little world, Mart. If there's a Venusian around, he sure knows his way."

"Data on Callisto? What kind?"

"A detailed map of Comprotown, showing every building. A full schedule of freighter hops both ways to Jupe and Earth. Details of shipments. That sort of thing."

"Holy stars! But why should a pirate be interested in ore?"

"Don't imagine he is. Or in Comprotown, either. I'd say from the papers, it was precautionary information. We don't keep our operations a secret here. He could have picked it up from any magazine article describing Comprotown in detail."

"But I still don't see—"

"The Ganymede jewel shipments, Mart. I'd say he was bound for Gany and his ship went blooie while he was scudding past Callisto. He got pulled down here and just barely made a landing he could walk away from. I'm afraid there'll be trouble."

Mart whistled. "Well, the Director's due now. He'll want a search organized and—Wait, here he is. Tell it over again, Cap, and you'll be reporting direct. . . . Listen to this, Director."

The tall slender figure of Director Barrow stood impassively beside Mart's desk and listened to a repetition of Wayne's report. Not a flicker of expression passed over his gaunt face.

As Wayne finished, the Director asked, "Is he armed? Anything taken from the ship's equipment, Captain?"

"Looks intact, but he probably has sidearms. All the pirates carry them. One funny thing, Director. The timer robot has been removed from the control panel. What on Callisto would he want with a loose timer?"

"Report back to headquarters immediately, Captain Wayne," Director Barrow ordered.

The hum of the carrier wave died and Mart clicked off the set. Then, belatedly, he stood up and saluted. "Anything I can do, sir? Everything's set for the freighters to clear as usual, so I'm more or less free—"

Barrow nodded. "Very good, Wells. You may go to the field and direct a search of the freighters. The Venusian's first thought will be to get away, and he may already be stowed in one of—"

A dry voice interrupted from behind the Director's back. "But the Venusian would not do anything so obvious, Director Barrow."

Mart whirled around. Barrow turned slowly and with dignity.

It was the tall man dressed in the uniform of a smelting plant worker who had spoken. But he wasn't dark-haired any more. Still seated, he was smiling at them sardonically as he fanned himself with a black wig he had just removed. The top of his head was as smooth as a billiard ball, and dead white. There was a line of demarcation where the dye he had applied to his face came to an end.

He had removed the tinted glasses too, and the blank-surfaced gray eyeballs showed why they had been worn. Now that the simple disguise of wig and glasses was removed, Mart noted some of the other distinguishing features that marked the Venusian. The general flatness of the face and flat unconvoluted ears. The six-fingered hands that had probably been thrust into the pockets of the stolen uniform.

The Venusian glanced down at the wig and glasses. "Standard equipment," he explained. "I always carry them in my ship and they've come in handy before."

He rose and bowed mockingly. "My name is Tar Norn, and your supposition that I am a pirate is correct. But I assure you that my visit here is accidental and I have no designs on Comprotown."

Tar Norn! The most vicious and notorious of the pirates, and the most ruthless killer of them all. Mart hastily jerked open the drawer of his desk and pulled out a hand-blaster. He started the formula: "Under authority of the Interplanetary Council, I arrest you, to be held for trial—"

The sardonic smile did not fade from the pirate's thin lips. He rose and extended his arms upward. "I am unarmed," he cut in. "It will help our discussion if you will verify that."

"—before the Supreme Council on Earth," Mart finished. Then, glancing sidewise at Director Barrow and seeing him nod, he stepped forward warily. Venusians, he knew, were both fast and tricky. Watching every move, he completed the search. Tar Norn carried no weapons.

Why, Mart wondered, had the pirate walked openly into headquarters and given himself up? Obviously, Tar Norn had something up his sleeve. But—

Director Barrow spoke coldly, as Mart stepped back, still covering the Venusian with the blaster. "Tar Norn, you speak of 'our discussion.' There is nothing to discuss. You will be sent to Earth."

The pirate's face became vicious. "I do not think so," he snapped. "I have taken a hostage. It was quite dark—your tiny Callisto in eclipse of its huge primary—when I was forced down. But darkness means nothing to a Venusian. You Earthmen play a strange game with cardboard rectangles. To use its language, Director Barrow, I have an ace in the hole."

Tar Norn sat down again and folded his six-fingered hands quite calmly. Light from the ceiling overhead seemed to cast a malignant glow on his dead-white scalp.

"Your daughter, Director," he continued. "If you wish to see her again, you will give me a ship, your *fastest* ship."

There was a moment of dead, utter silence. Then Director Barrow leaned over the desk and flicked the key of the communicator. "Control? Get my—get Leah Barrow at once. Ring her room. If no answer there, get my housekeeper. This is Director Barrow."

"Your fastest ship," repeated the Venusian. "Well stocked with supplies. Enough to take me to—to a place in the Asteroid belt. I shall be too late now to carry out my original plans on Ganymede."

The office door opened and Captain Wayne came in, followed by Roger Corey. Their eyes widened as they saw the Venusian. Wayne's hand darted toward his holster, then relaxed as he saw Mart's blaster trained on the pirate.

He faced Director Barrow and saluted.

"Captain," Barrow ordered, "you will form a search party at once—every available man and means. We must search all of Callisto within—" he made a rapid mental calculation "—about fifty miles. You will be searching for my daughter."

The captain stiffened. Before he could reply the carrier wave hummed and a feminine voice, that of an elderly woman, came over the communicator. "Director Barrow? Leah isn't here. I looked in her room and her bed is disarranged as though she left suddenly. She always makes it herself as soon as she gets up."

"Anything to point to when she left, Mrs. Andrews?"

"Not exactly, sir. The alarm was set for six and it was still buzzing. Her bed isn't very mussed; it looks like she got up again almost right after she retired. I don't understand."

Director Barrow's face was bleak. His voice sounded like the drip of water from melting ice. "Clothing?" he asked.

"Her lightweight spacesuit is gone. Apparently she put it on over her sleeping pajamas, for they aren't here. Is there anything I can do, sir? I'm worried; she hasn't ever—"

"That will be all, Mrs. Andrews," Barrow replied. "I'll let you know if there is anything."

He turned to Captain Wayne. "Use this set, Captain. Get Communications to send out a general alarm and assembly. You can make all necessary arrangements right here."

Wayne crossed to the communicator, and began to issue rapid instructions.

"Tell them to hurry," the Venusian cut in mockingly. "They have until nine-thirty o'clock."

Mart Wells glanced fearfully at the dial of the chronometer. It was eight-forty now. He turned and caught the Director's glance. *"The timer!"* he said grimly. "Captain Wayne said it was missing from the wrecked ship. He must have—"

The Venusian was grinning. "Exactly. The timer. And a pound of uranite. That gives you fifty minutes to search Callisto. It would be wiser to spend the time getting a ship ready for me instead."

The silence of the office was broken only by the low voice of Captain Wayne giving orders into the communicator. Abruptly he turned to his superior. His face was white.

"Search is on, sir. But if he isn't lying, there's a chance in a million. Less than an hour, and the area to be covered is—"

Barrow was looking straight ahead, and not a muscle of his face moved until he spoke. "I'm afraid he isn't bluffing. No reason why he should be. Leah is gone and the timer is gone. And a pirate ship would have uranite."

"The ship?" asked Tar Norn. "It will take some time to fuel it and—"

Director Barrow's voice was positive. "There will be no ship for you, Tar Norn."

Roger Corey's voice cut in, jerkily. "Let me work on him, sir. Me and Wayne. Maybe we can make him talk."

Barrow shook his head. "No use, Corey. Venusians don't mind pain as much as Earthmen. They almost like it. You could take him apart, and he wouldn't talk."

The pirate's smile faded. "It will take half an hour to prepare the ship, Director Barrow. Better not stall too long."

Mart said, his voice urgent. "But, sir, *Leah!* What's one pirate compared to—"

Barrow's face was granite-like. "He's killed hundreds of people. If we release him, he'll kill hundreds more. One life cannot weigh against that. Corey, take him away. Lock him up until the next ship leaves for Earth."

Mart's fists were clenched, his fingernails biting into the palms. But he knew Barrow was right; that he couldn't possibly take any other course and be worthy of his post. One life couldn't weigh against the many lives that meeting the pirate's terms would mean. That was where Tar Norn had miscalculated. A Venusian didn't understand responsibility to society, nor any higher ideal than self-interest.

Tar Norn tossed the wig and glasses to the floor as Corey took his arm. His pupilless eyes seemed to glow with anger.

"You won't murder your own daughter, Director. This is a bluff. But mine isn't. She dies at nine-thirty unless you find her. I swear that by the *Eternal Varga.*"

Mart cursed. Fists balled, he lunged toward the Venusian. Barrow put a hand on his arm. "Don't, Wells. That's up to the Interplanetary Council."

"But he's *not* bluffing," Mart raved. "Leah will surely die at nine-thirty. That damned oath. *Varga.* It's the only thing a Venusian is afraid of. He isn't—" His voice broke.

Corey started off with the Venusian.

Barrow said, "Yes, he's telling the truth. But we have some time yet. Maybe the search—"

Mart strode to the window and looked out so the others wouldn't see his face. Less than three-quarters of an hour to search all of Callisto within a radius of fifty miles!

Through the pane he saw figures in groups of three searching the streets and buildings of Comprotown. That part of the search wouldn't be difficult. But the hills and the caves, and with only two autogiros. If she was there, out of sight in one of the caves, where the cruising ships couldn't see her . . .

Her father was right, but—The picture of Leah Barrow, smiling as he had last seen her, seemed to blur out the view from the window. Her impertinent little tilted nose, the soft tempting contour of her lips, the deep blueness of her eyes.

He whirled from the window and began pacing the floor, trying to think of something they could do that wasn't being done. Again at the communicator, Captain Wayne was barking questions.

"All available men and women are combing the town, sir," he reported, "with orders to break down any doors that are locked, to stop at nothing."

"And outside, Captain?"

"The two giros are our only real hope. But the men from the smelting plant are working afoot out of town. By nine-thirty they'll have covered a radius of about five miles."

Corey returned, slamming the door viciously behind him. "Maybe we could trick him, sir," he suggested. "Pretend we'll give him a ship if he'll—"

"A Venusian wouldn't trust his own mother," Barrow snapped. "He'd insist on taking off first and then radioing back where she is. And don't think he wouldn't check the fuel tanks."

"I wish you'd let me and Wayne work on him, anyway."

Director Barrow didn't answer.

Mart growled, "If Leah dies, I'm going to take that filthy pirate and—"

Wayne's voice was bitter. "Venusians can't help what they are. Blame the Earth council that sold them those ships. If they had used more sense, there wouldn't be a Venusian off Venus."

Mart nodded. "If the council hadn't pulled that boner twenty years before, there would be no trouble with the Venusians."

Venusians were, compared to Earth standards, a strange combination of genius and idiocy. Brilliant mathematicians, they had no mechanical ingenuity whatever. Linguists who could speak any language fluently after hearing it a few hours, not one of them could create a child's wind-up toy. Knowing the laws of leverage, they constructed their buildings by manual labor alone. Able to operate any machine as long as it was in good working order, they couldn't as much as figure out how to repair a clogged fuel-line.

Even the pirates based on some of the bigger

Asteroids had to depend upon a few renegade Earthmen to keep their ships in running order. And if one went blah away from base, it was a gone ship as far as they were concerned. Probably the trouble that had forced Tar Norn down on Callisto had been a minor matter that any Earthman could have taken in his stride. But to Tar Norn it meant a new ship or nothing.

The thought of ships reminded him of the freighters. "Cap," he asked Wayne, "have the freighters been searched thoroughly?"

Wayne nodded. "Rocket tubes and all. Even broke open the ore drums. I presume you'll want them to clear on schedule?"

Director Barrow nodded. "The crews?" he asked. "In the search or standing by?"

"Standing by for departure as usual, Director. A few men one way or the other—"

Barrow nodded, glancing at the chronometer. Mart knew what he was thinking. Less than half an hour now. And, unless the searchers by some miracle found Leah Barrow, it would all be over before the ten o'clock clearance of the first freighter. And the freighters hadn't missed a clearance in ten years.

The carrier waved hummed again. "Central Communications reporting. Most searchers in the town have reported in. No results. Those outside reaching points three miles out."

The communicator faded. Mart clenched his fists against the futility of that search. Three miles! The strong Venusian, in the light gravity of Callisto, probably had eight or ten hours of darkness to carry his burden. He could easily have covered twenty to forty miles, in any direction. Possibly even more. And the chance of an autogiro—

Obviously, Wayne had been thinking the same thing. "He timed his arrival," he said bitterly. "He gave us less than an hour. He'd certainly have put her outside walking range within that length of time. And with all the caves around, thousands of them, would he have put her where a giro could spot anything?"

Mart glanced at Barrow. The Director was sitting as immobile as a statue. His eyes were closed and every muscle of his thin face was tense. Probably he was trying not to look at the chronometer on the wall. It was nine-fifteen.

The office door opened and three uniformed mechanics from the field stood in the doorway. The foremost of them saluted. "This entire building has been searched twice except this office. I presume—"

Director Barrow opened his eyes and stood up. "Don't presume anything. Search here, too."

The men came in and began a detailed but fruitless search. Nobody spoke until they left.

The chronometer said twenty minutes after nine now. Ten minutes to go, if the timer had been accurately set. But could it have been set wrong? Venusians were lousy mechanics. Maybe—

Mart became aware that he was holding his breath for the sound of a distant explosion. Yes, from whatever point Tar Norn could have hidden his hostage, the sound of a pound of uranite exploding would carry back to Comprotown.

He sat down at his desk again. In front of him were the signed clearance papers for the freighters. In half an hour he'd take out the papers for the first freighter. But before that half hour was up—

He twisted a pencil between his fingers, held himself rigid to keep from turning and looking at the chronometer again. It hadn't been over a minute since he sat down—why torture himself by looking again? But each minute now seemed both a flash and an eternity.

He turned over the sheaf of papers and drew a little square on the blank reverse side of the bottom one. That was Comprotown. He made a dot an inch or two away. That was the point where Tar Norn's ship had wrecked itself in landing.

He drew a line from the point to the square. That was Tar Norn coming in to the town. That would have been about ten hours ago.

Then, from the information about Callisto and Comprotown that had been in the papers in Tar Norn's ship, the pirate had found the home of the director. He would have had no trouble finding Leah's room. Venusians could see in the dark and walk as silently as cats. He would undoubtedly have drugged Leah into unconsciousness, probably without awakening her, since there had been no sign of a struggle. He'd put her into the lightweight spacesuit.

Why? Undoubtedly it indicated that she would be outdoors. During the Callisto day, it would have been unnecessary. But an unconscious Earthwoman would freeze to death in the cold dark period of Callisto's eclipse behind Big Jupe.

What then? The Venusian left, carrying her—

He threw down the pencil and began to pace the room again. His muscles were tense from listening. How many minutes? He didn't want to know; dared not look.

But Tar Norn must have planned it all before he left the wrecked ship. Otherwise he wouldn't have taken the timer and—

Would he have rigged the time-bomb first, or after he had kidnapped Leah? And how? The timer itself would not have provided the concussion to set off the uranite. He'd have needed a battery, a spark-coil, and—

But Venusians weren't mechanics.

They didn't understand machines, or electricity, or even simple clockworks, brilliant as their strange minds were in other ways.

Tar Norn could have set the timer all right. For that matter, he could calculate an orbit and make settings for space flight. But he couldn't have made a time-bomb, even with the timer. He couldn't have rigged a circuit that would set off a cap! And, Mart realized suddenly, the timer itself would be an electrical—not a clockwork—gadget. Once disconnected from the now broken dynamo of the ship, Tar Norn couldn't have made it run at all!

A momentary surge of elation swept Mart. Tar Norn must have been bluffing! Then he remembered: a Venusian might murder his own family, but he would never swear to an untruth by the *Eternal Varga*. That one superstition, or religion, as they looked upon it, was binding beyond all else. And Tar Norn had sworn by that oath that Leah Barrow would die at nine-thirty unless—

Mart looked at the chronometer. It was twenty-six minutes past nine. He caught a glimpse of Director Barrow's face. It looked like the face of a dead man. Barrow had obviously given up all hope and waited only for the four minutes to pass.

The carrier wave hummed. All of them started, but the voice from the communicator merely reported, "All Comprotown reports in. All negative. Giros report nothing. Foot parties five miles out. Reports negative."

Three minutes to go. Mart could see by the attitude of the others that they were bracing themselves for the sound of an explosion. All of them had liked, or loved, Leah Barrow. Mart had a momentary vision of her again, and remembered the electric thrill that had run through him when she had placed her hand on his arm, just a few days ago, and told him that she did care for him, well, a little anyway—

But, if Tar Norn couldn't have rigged a time-bomb, how could he have arranged for Leah to die at nine-thirty?

He saw again the corpse-like face of the Director. Yes. They had all been wrong in thinking that nothing mattered to Barrow more than the schedules—*Schedules!* There had been departure schedules among the papers in Tar Norn's ship. Could he have—

With a sudden intake of breath that was almost a gasp, Mart whirled and ran to the communicator. The others looked at him, startled. Mart was yelling at the mike even before he got near enough to it to talk in a normal voice. "Control! Emergency! Get *Jupe Freighter One! Tell him not to test his tubes.* Not to touch a lever!"

Then he was racing out of the door and across the field to where the big ugly freighter was up on the racks over the blasting pits. He wasn't counting on that message through the communicator.

Out of breath, he hammered on the steel door and yanked at the handle until the pilot opened it from within.

"Hold everything," Mart yelled at him. "Don't try the test blasts!"

Whether Mart was right or wrong, there needn't be any hurry now, but he was already lowering himself into the ash-filled blasting pit under the rocket tubes of the freighter. Carefully, he groped among the ashes from previous blast-offs, ignoring the light soft ash that flew up into his face.

A hand touched heavy cloth, and the other found

smooth transpariplast, the helmet of a spacesuit. Gently, he lifted the unconscious body of Leah Barrow and handed her up to the men looking down from the rim of the pit.

Ten minutes later, back in the office, Leah was reacting to the antidote Doc Rogers had just administered. A glance at her face had told the medico that the drug had been Venusian tragweed.

Mart was still answering questions. ". . . Sure, Tar Norn knew that. Every ship in the system makes its trial blasts just half an hour before take-off. It's a fixed convention. Rocket captains do everything according to a rigid schedule. And we were looking for a time-bomb so we'd never think of the blasting pits. But Tar Norn couldn't have rigged a time-bomb. We didn't think of that when we found the timer was gone. He'd just thrown it away—"

Someone was wringing his hand, and he saw it was Director Barrow. "Mart!" Barrow's voice wasn't cold and distant now; all the ice had melted. "I can't begin to tell you how much—If there is any reward I can possibly offer you—"

Mart Wells grinned. "—unto your daughter and half of your kingdom, as they used to say in stories? Well, sir, I don't know what I'd do with half of Callisto, but as for the other part of it—"

He turned back to the awakening girl. Director Barrow's answer was cinched, of course, but Leah—? Well, he'd have to ask her again.

But probably she wasn't up to that just yet, even

though her eyes were open now and she was smiling at him. He'd have to give her time, of course, before he asked her. Lots of time. Say, five minutes, or maybe three.

Mars-Station

BETTYANN KEVLES

"OHHH . . ." Ann wanted to scream. Now she would have to repeat the whole experiment. Pursing her lips, she peeled off the labels and put them on the right containers. How had Psychic-Conditioning ever let that practical-joker into Mars-Station?

"Oh Rolf," she thought. "Won't you ever grow up?"

Ann straightened the lab and eased herself swimmingly through the hatch into her sleep-cocoon. Some televiews were ready in the screen. She lay back and switched it on.

Mars glowed dull red three hundred miles below her window. A meteor streaked by, but Ann didn't notice. Her eyes were fastened on the green trees and graceful students who swarmed beneath them at University.

"Always signaling the next step," Ann thought

sadly. Ten years earlier, when TASS (The Terran Association for Space Scientists) had removed her from home in Dabney, Vermont, they had also prepared her. Then she had been conditioned, and trained, and educated for the semi-isolation of the laboratory-satellite. It had worked pretty well. Today Ann was the oldest human being to have survived, her faculties undamaged, in space. And now TASS had decided it was time to bring her back. That explained the beaming of University televiews.

She stared at the crowds on the screen. No older than she, the earth-reared students seemed casually confident; they could have belonged to a different species. Ann wondered how she would ever be able to live with them after six years in space.

Beneath Ann, if you cared to use such a meaningless term in space, Rolf also examined University views. He, too, knew the ways of TASS and he was as apprehensive as Ann. A decade ago, when TASS had taken him from the sleepy town of Bormes on the Swiss border to enroll in The Academy, he had been reluctant to leave earth, and now it was time to return.

Student life didn't frighten Rolf as it did Ann, nor did the masses of strangers. On the contrary, Rolf had been dreaming of his triumphal return, of his heroic return, ever since his first day in space. It was because of that dream that he had consented to leave the pleasures of home, and that same dream held him where he was. He did not want to return —not yet.

"FOURTH-MEAL SERVED IN NEXUS CENTRAL," the intercom announced.

From their quarters in the arms of the artificial satellite, the crew assembled. Ann and Hannah entered first; Rolf and Chang followed. They paid court to an antiquated system of etiquette particularly at odds with the absolute equality that existed in their laboratories. The boys helped the girls into the magnetic chairs. Ann winced. Rolf always pulled the belt too tight, then released it after he saw her pain. And Ann never complained. Then he seated himself. Slowly, following an intricate ritual, they sipped the dull series of flavorless recycled foods that was all the four young scientists had known for almost a third of their lives.

"Our University-views arrived." Rolf told the junior team. "I guess that gives Ann and me at the most three months before we leave."

"Oh!" Hannah started, and inadvertently released her plastistraw which began to drift towards Chang. "How I'll miss you, both of you! But of course you must be so excited, going home at last." Hannah had been at Mars-Station only two years and still felt homesick for her family in Jerusalem.

"I'm more nervous than excited," Ann confessed. She seldom bothered to disguise her feelings from the others. "I just can't imagine myself walking on grass, weighted down like one of our magnetized shoes."

"Are you sure that's what's really bothering you?" Rolf knew her too well.

Ann leaned inward. "I guess not. That's just part of it. You remember how shy I was when we entered the Academy?"

Rolf smiled. Ann had been the funniest little girl. He could see her now, dropping things all over the place, and then cleaning up his mess along with her own every time. Poor Ann, she always seemed to be waiting for things to happen to her. "I remember," Rolf said.

"At the Academy they just pushed mathematics and biology and conditioning, and more conditioning, biology and mathematics. I'm afraid I won't be able to talk to other students again. And what will they think of me? How will I look to them?" She shook her heavy mane of brown hair and it floated in an aureole around her head. "And how will I move, like a crab? You know we've all been weightless since age twelve! Maybe I'll just teeter like a baby." She giggled, but the sound soon turned into sobs. "Oh, I don't really know, but I'm afraid I'll hate it back there!"

Rolf grinned. "Well Ann, we'll be returning together. Maybe we can enroll together at University. Then we can relearn to walk holding hands."

"Please don't tease." Chang spoke quietly. "You know they won't let you near each other after you return. The TASS contract has us sharing our experience throughout the whole international community. Besides, you'll probably never want to see each other again. Six years in this confinement is enough for a lifetime."

Ann and Rolf knew Chang was right. Of the half-dozen pairs of scientists who had come and gone from Mars-Station, these two had had the least in common. Ann feared Rolf. He was smart, but unpredictable. She knew his lust for fame, and his rush for results which often made his work sloppy and inaccurate. Even at the Academy, he had once stolen someone else's lab-notes in order to finish first. He had won, and the other student had been dismissed when it had looked to TASS as if the runner-up had done the cheating.

"What bothers me about returning now," Rolf admitted, "is that I haven't solved it. I hate to go back empty-handed. I mean all these years here, the years of my youth—sacrificed—and for what—for nothing!"

"How can you say that?" Hannah was appalled. "You and Ann have done a lot. You've managed to feed your test-animals from Mars-food cultivated in the modular-radiation-vehicle, and that proves it will be economically feasible to support colonization."

"But colonization by whom?" Rolf asked sarcastically, "by children? The big question is still open. And that's the real reason we're here, isn't it?"

Hannah had to agree. Sixty years earlier, after the first Space Station had been established between earth and its moon, a strange phenomenon had developed. "Glandular Disorientation (GD), space-sickness affecting the nervous system, so severe that it totally incapacitated everyone who remained weightless longer than five months. And five months is not enough time in Space to develop a colony.

"GD only affects adults, isn't that right?" Hannah asked.

"Well, only mature humans over the age of about eighteen. That's why TASS began. The Association chooses youngsters between nine and eleven and then prepares them to staff the Mars-Station. With four to six good working years, we should have been able to use the perfect vacuum of space to solve lots of scientific problems."

Chang spoke thoughtfully. "We must hurry. Earth's population is growing too fast. Colonization of Mars is more urgent today even than two years ago when I arrived. And the Psychic-research team still insists that only a full-spectrum of ages, infants through the aged, can establish an emotionally stable colony."

"I think three months may be enough time, Chang." Ann spoke softly. "I'm working on some algae you brought back from your last descent exploration of the upper strata, and I've separated out one very simple cellular formation. So far it's been successful on Alfred."

Chang and Hannah laughed. Ann kept test beagles and one of them was always called Alfred.

Rolf looked startled. How could Ann have done it without his knowledge? Ann. Selfless, clumsy, denigrating Ann! Ann the prize-winner of all time? Absurd!

Hannah bubbled enthusiastically, her English

fluent at last after years of adjustment to the international language. "So if it works on Alfred, that means it will work on people?" Hannah was an astronomer (TASS sent out geologists and physicists as well as biochemists) and sometimes she found the ways of her colleagues totally incomprehensible.

"Hopefully." Rolf had regained his equilibrium. "All mammals seem to suffer from GD. We've never tried whales or elephants in space, but all small mammals have experienced it. Of course mammals vary. Now Ann's beagles have certain systems uncannily similar to ours. My chimpanzees are very humanoid in other ways, although now I think I might have been better off with puppies."

He tried to sound gay, concealing his own sense of frustration, of loss. "Well, Ann old girl, are you prepared to be queen of the May, you know, to accept fame and fortune?"

"You mean prepared to be the biggest freak in the circus?" Ann cried out. "I wish I had never come here. I want to be alone." And she unhooked her belt and pushed with that swimming motion back through the hatch into her quarters.

Safe inside the lab, she lost the timidity that dominated her relationships with people. She was neither shy nor awkward with her test tubes. At eighteen, she was one of the most completely accomplished organic chemists that the world scientific community had been able to produce. And she hadn't let them down.

She ran through a final series of tests on Algae M'

and fed some to Alfred. Alfred was exactly eighteen months older than he had a right to be. He had outlived his brothers and sisters and even his first set of pups.

Ann entered the time into her lab manual and prepared the mini-capsule in which Alfred would soar earthward after the next sleep-cycle. She toured the lab, strapping everything into place, and then slipped through the hatch into the sleep-cocoon where she attached the medic-computer to her head, chest and feet, locked them into place, and closed her eyes.

"Can I borrow a beaker?" Rolf's voice on the intercom caught her as she was dozing off.

"Sure," she murmured, as Rolf entered the adjoining lab. By the time he had found the beaker and begun to explore, Ann had fallen asleep.

Rolf hadn't been inside Ann's quarters since the first years when they had worked together. That was until Ann had discovered what Rolf knew all along. Conditioning was not fool-proof. It depended on the kind of personality you started out with. Ann followed all the rules TASS deemed necessary on the satellite. Rolf, on the other hand, had not changed since his Academy adventures. He followed only those rules that seemed to agree with his needs.

Life could be dull at Mars-Station, so a few years ago Rolf had gone to a great deal of trouble to liven things up. He had rearranged the whole lab, making floors walls, ceilings floors, and rebolting everything in the appropriate place. It had been very funny, like a madhouse at a carnival. But it had ruined Ann's carefully controlled experiment which did not need gravity but which did depend on total rest.

That had ended all future collaboration. And Rolf had never apologised, because he had never understood Ann's anger.

Rolf saw the green test tubes suspended above Ann's lab manual. He glanced at them several times, and then gave in to curiosity and removed the heavy magnet that held the notebook to the wall. He had little trouble following Ann's logic, after all they had worked together for a long time. He didn't bother following the complicated equations; Ann's math was better than his. From what he did read, however, he had to conclude that Ann's speculation had been modest. The thick green liquid in the test tubes most certainly held the hopes of Humanity.

Unprocessed Martian algae dangled in a chrysalsphere nearby. It looked so humble in its simplicity. "Organic, of course," Rolf mumbled, staring back at the test tubes.

He stared into the green mist until he felt he was floating inside a mint sea. "Wonder what it tastes like?" He giggled at his thought. He should never find out. It was against every scientific precept he had ever learned at the Academy, against every rule of common sense, and against the TASS regulations for Mars-Station. No human being would taste that liquid until every test-animal had been exhausted, and then the chosen human being would be one especially selected for the trial.

Rolf lifted the test tube from its armature and held it to a source of light. It was really quite beautiful, he thought.

He uncorked the tube and held it to his nose. It didn't have an odor. He knew that what he was doing was wrong. He shouldn't have touched Ann's solution, but he didn't stop. He tilted the test tube toward his lips. He felt scared, but at the same time exhilarated. This was a great gamble, but wasn't life made of gambles? If he didn't drink, someone else would eventually test the algae, someone else, after years of testing, someone else would be the first.

He sucked a huge mouthful of the bitter fluid, and as he swallowed he could almost hear the voices shouting, the applause. How they loved him, Rolf, the first human being to live into maturity, in space! He drank.

Eight hours later Rolf sipped equally bitter reconstituted orange juice at First-meal, the most important of the four eating-sessions that punctuated the fourteen hour wake cycle. During First-meal the youth team held its daily exchange with the Newfoundland lab, by video, to the entire world, or at least to those people at home interested enough to tune in.

Usually the crew arrived in Nexus together, but this First-meal Ann was late.

"I've been searching my lab for the second test tube, but it's gone. I can't understand it!" She looked upset, too.

"Maybe Alfred got hungry and drank some more," Rolf volunteered.

"How did you know that that is what Alfred's been taking?" Ann shot back.

"Quiet! Discus is lighting," Chang interrupted.

Ann stared at Rolf but he pretended to be searching for the recessed button in the arm of his chair. A foolish pretense, Ann thought; they had been pressing that button daily since their first cycle at the station. Resigned to waiting, Ann pressed her own button and the chair tilted, leaving First-meal behind at a 45 degree angle.

"Good day to all of you." Dr. Randall's black face smiled at them. That meant Thursday. Every day a different member of the terrestrial lab spoke, setting a pattern to their lives that the lack of sunrise-sunset had taken away.

"There isn't much news today," Dr. Randall continued. "The U.S. table-tennis team went down to defeat again, in Peking."

Chang beamed. He had first tried playing the traditional game at Mars-Station but had soon devised a variation using four balls that made more sense in the absence of gravity.

"In Jerusalem students have organized a three-day camel race from Cairo to Tel-Aviv and one hundred camels are still walking."

Hannah had raised a baby camel before TASS had spotted her and whisked her off to the Academy. Now she slept with a small stuffed dromedary in her cocoon.

"Let's see, Ann—" Dr. Randall continued, "your family will be here to speak to you Sunday. They want to know which campus of University you've chosen to attend. You too, Rolf. All Europe is waiting to see which city you'll be in, Paris, Moscow, Berlin, Helsinki?"

Ann and Rolf nodded nervously.

"Now it's Station-relay. We can accept technical information immediately. If you want a personal relay, we can arrange for a closed transmission later today."

Ann started to ask for a personal relay but Rolf blurted his news to the world before she had her words ready.

"We've done it! We've found it. Ann and I. She's isolated an ordinary strain of upper strata Martian algae and metabolized it with canine pituitary extract. Alfred beagle has been mature for over a year and he shows no sign of deterioration. All we needed to finish testing was a human test-animal, and so, to save time for everyone—I volunteered! I took some of the vile-tasting fluid myself. Now all we have to do is watch my progress to see how successful we are in halting GD."

Silence greeted Rolf, not the applause he expected. He had broken every scientific procedure and had not bothered to consult the lab in Newfoundland.

"I took it myself," he repeated. "Instead of going to University, I'll stay here. With your permission, of course, I thought that I could continue work at the Station for about two years to prove the effectiveness of what we call Algae M'."

Even the golden glow in the disk could not disguise Dr. Randall's expression. He was stunned. At Mars-Station too there was a startled silence. Ann's face registered outrage mixed with something else—fear. Chang drew into himself and away from Rolf. Hannah alone looked pleased.

Ann spoke first. She knew she could not accuse Rolf in front of the planet-wide audience, nor could she condemn him privately, not now, not considering the risk he had taken.

"Dr. Randall." Ann always spoke softly, almost in a whisper; people all over the earth bent closer to their sets to hear. "Dr. Randall, Alfred is on his way earthside now. I, ah, we weren't certain how the enzyme would affect Alfred's metabolism under gravitational conditions. He should splash down Wednesday, near Tahiti, I believe. If you quarantine him for six weeks and perform the complete test series, we should have a better idea then of the extent of our success."

Dr. Randall took refuge in scientific detail and he used the rest of the transmission to ascertain the exact nature of the substance Ann had manufactured. When Discus blinked off, the four members of the space lab found themselves facing each other in the most awkward moment they had spent together since the younger team had arrived two years earlier to replace the then senior team that was being cycled back to earth.

"I didn't know you worked together?" Hannah said innocently in a tone that would have sounded sarcastic from anyone else. A theoretician with her telescope, Hannah was ignorant of the way biochemists worked in their laboratories.

"Well, we don't usually collaborate," Ann said bitterly.

"Ann, what can I say?" Rolf twisted his hands as he spoke. "I should have told you right away. I meant to. Besides, someone had to test the stuff on a human. Oh Ann, can't you ever understand? I had to be a part of it. I *needed* to be a part."

Ann understood very well. Rolf's weaknesses were as familiar to her as her own.

Rolf changed his approach. "Anyway, there's plenty left in the other tube. Why don't you have a drink too? We can remain up here together another couple of years. That'll save them sending a vehicle just for you."

Ann didn't answer. She turned away.

"Come on Ann, stay. You were right about University. You'll be the laughing-stock. Can't you see them pointing? Oh sure, at first they'll be curious, but after the novelty wears off you'll just be the space-nut in residence."

Ann turned on him angrily. "And that's exactly why I've got to return. If I stayed here, I'd always wonder. Besides Rolf, if Algae M' works, I can always come back if I don't like earth."

Rolf's eyes narrowed. "What do you mean *if?"*

"Forget it."

"Forget what?"

"Never mind!" Ann raised her voice in a hard tone unusual for her. "I'll see you at University in two years, I'm sure I will." She would not mention her doubts to Rolf, not unless she had to, and she hoped that never happened. Slowly, she left Nexus.

Chang spoke. "What you did is wrong, Rolf. Until you can understand that, we will never be able to continue working together as a unit." He left too.

"I understand." Hannah touched Rolf's shoulder. "It was too big a temptation. And you really did short-cut all that red-tape choosing an earth subject would have entailed. I think that in the long-run, humanity will thank you for your action. Anyway Rolf, I'm glad that you'll be here at the Station another two years."

Alfred was on his way to earth so Ann did not return to her lab until Saturday. But something was bothering her about those equations. She reread her notes and procedure several times, and then she went through the complicated mathematics. Finally, during what would have been the early hours of the morning Sunday, if there had been a morning, she found her error. It was a simple one, the kind she used to make at the Academy that had set all the others, especially Rolf, laughing.

By feeding the solution directly into Alfred's stomach, it had mixed with gastric enzymes which had in turn reacted chemically with those enzymes and changed its chemistry. But if she were to inject it directly into the pituitary gland, she saw, it could go to work directly, unaltered, undiluted.

Ann chose Gladys, one of Alfred's daughters, and injected Algae M' directly into her pituitary gland. Then, for the first time in weeks, she relaxed, for a while.

Life at Mars-Station continued its normal routine, with one exception. At meal-times, total silence prevailed. Politeness continued, for this behavior had been successfully conditioned into them and they could not help it. But frankness was also part of their conditioning, and Ann especially did not want to tell Rolf about her mistake. She still hoped it wouldn't make any difference.

Then, at First-meal the next Thursday, Dr. Randall announced that Alfred had arrived and had been transported to Newfoundland. He appeared in good health and even, Dr. Randall quipped, sent his regards to the whole team at Mars-Station. Dr. Randall also delivered TASS's decision about Rolf. TASS was not at all pleased with his initiative, but since it was already an accomplished fact, they had decided to support him and allow him to remain at the Station an additional twenty-two months. As for Ann, they would send for her in six weeks.

Seventeen days later, at First-meal, they received the first news something had gone wrong. In his kennel in Newfoundland, Alfred had stopped eating.

Ann stopped eating too, and so did Rolf, until the medic-computer in their cocoons relayed the fact back to Newfoundland and they were directed, at the next First-meal relay, to resume ingestion—immediately.

"How do you feel Rolf?" Ann asked him then. "Do you think Algae M' has affected you at all?"

"Not really," Rolf pointed to his chin. "But my beard is growing rapidly so that proves I'm maturing and look," he held both arms out straight in front of him, "no shakes, no sign of GD."

Ann returned to her lab. Gladys seemed fine too, and she was getting older seven times faster than any human being could.

Two weeks later, more news.

Alfred had begun to lose his fur. They were still feeding him intravenously but he didn't seem to be responding.

Rolf entered Ann's lab that day. "What is it?" he demanded. "You know something you're not telling me. I have a right to know." His voice had risen in pitch and Ann sensed that beneath his flippant exterior, he was approaching hysteria.

"Well, I don't know how serious it is," she began,

excusing her lack of explanation. She took the manual off the wall where it hung suspended.

"It's here. You didn't follow all of my equations the night you took it, did you?"

"Of course not. You know how I hate detail work. Besides, you're the best mathematician here. Why check an Einstein?"

"Because 'Einsteins' make mistakes too. Remember all those whoppers I made at the Academy? You should remember, you made sure everyone else knew about them too."

"But you were only a kid then!" Rolf protested.

"Well, I haven't changed as much as you assumed. Look." She pointed to a set which she had circled in red. "There's the mistake. I found it later, but I had the feeling something was wrong before you drank it. Something just didn't seem right."

Rolf paled. "What does this mean?"

"I'm not sure." Ann's clear eyes searched his face, looking for reassurance. "I think it means that the solution can't be absorbed properly in the bloodstream. Since it combines with pituitary extract, and since it is the pituitary gland that controls growth and development in mammals, I think it means that the solution should be injected directly into the gland."

Rolf stared out the window into the stars. "What does this mean for me?"

"I don't know, Rolf. I really don't know."

Four weeks passed and everyone at Mars-Station tried to concentrate on other projects, but they really lived for the daily broadcast with its report on Alfred. He still lingered, but he had ceased all motion short of breathing.

At Mars-Station, Rolf felt fine. He'd let a beard grow to show the television audience how successfully he was weathering maturation. This was in brilliant contrast to Ann. She had begun experiencing the first signs of GD, nothing serious, or incurable, but enough to prove that TASS's timing about her return had been accurate. Their calculations had indicated that Rolf, too, should be experiencing some GD, but clearly, he was not.

The day the vehicle with Ann's replacement arrived, was the same day they learned of Alfred's death.

"Maybe it had nothing to do with Algae M'!" Rolf shouted into Discus. "He could have caught a virus, or got food poisoning. You can't say it killed him, you can't. Just look at me! I feel fine!"

"Rolf, we haven't had time to perform an autopsy on Alfred. We don't know the exact cause of death." The Newfoundland speaker spoke morosely.

When Ann arrived on earth a month later, the lab decided to inform Rolf, and the rest of the world, about the results of the autopsy.

As the team on Mars-Station watched Dr. Randall with Ann by his side, Rolf felt his flesh chill.

"The Algae M' affected a permanent change in Alfred beagle's bloodstream. The change adapted him to life as a mature animal in weightlessness, but the effect of gravity on him proved fatal. The change to his blood is a permanent change, and it is irreversible."

"But what about me!" Rolf cried out.

"I'm afraid the medic-computer indicates that your blood has experienced the same reaction. You can continue your work as a scientist at Mars-Station for the rest of your life. But any attempt to return to earth, I'm afraid, would prove fatal."

Rolf knew they were right. He ached to pound his hands and feet on the ground and cry out for help. But he knew he would never again feel the release of pounding in gravity, or of seeing a sunset.

Rolf watched Discus along with millions on earth who watched their video sets as Ann displayed Gladys, alive and wagging her tail. Gladys who proved that by direct injection Algae M' was indeed the cure for GD.

A prisoner of space, Rolf watched Ann, many times, with Gladys always by her side, as she accepted the Medal of Freedom, the Copley Medal of the Royal Society, the Nobel Prize.

He watched her as she acquired poise and grace, a world traveler, not a freak, but a beloved heroine.

The Mars Jar

A. M. LIGHTNER

THE jar stood on a back shelf in the laboratory, where for some reason it had missed being cleaned out when the experiment was abandoned. For the past two weeks, whenever Andrew Elliott needed anything from that corner of the lab, he had made a practice of walking past and looking up at the jar. Something, it seemed to him, might be growing there.

The Mars experiment was not his baby. It was the work of the eminent Dr. L. L. Booth, who left the base soon after Andrew came to work there.

He remembered the project being talked about at the time. A number of airtight jars had been arranged with red sandstone or lava soil in the bottoms. Each jar received its complement of seeds, spores or soil bacteria, and then the air had been pumped out until only a very thin atmosphere remained, such as is found several miles above Mt.

Everest, or, theoretically, on the surface of the planet Mars.

The temperature had been reduced to that of the red planet, and only the amount of sunlight allowed that daily reaches our distant neighbor. When everything possible had been done to duplicate the environment of Mars, the jars had been watched to see if any life form could endure and develop in these rugged conditions.

The idea had immediately aroused the young scientist's interest, but unfortunately by the time he joined the Army's space research group, the experiment had been written off as "results negative." Andrew found himself working under one of the naturalized German scientists, transferred to fill Dr. Booth's place.

Dr. Karl von Plank was a difficult man to work with. Not only was his English often difficult to follow, but he insisted on prompt and exact fulfilment of his orders, and he was not interested in anyone else's ideas. He had ordered the Mars jars cleaned out shortly after he took charge of the group, and it was only because this one was hidden behind some other paraphernalia that it had not suffered a like fate.

Perhaps it was because Dr. von Plank, a German of the old order, was so meticulous and pedantic that young Dr. Elliott found it necessary to enliven his days by occasionally peering at Dr. Booth's imaginative experiment. Dr. von Plank had dismissed the whole thing in his usual positive manner when it was first brought to his attention.

"We are not here to indulge in fairy-tale dreams," he said. "We are here to develop diets for astronauts. They must take everything with them. Everyone knows that nothing grows on Mars."

The first time Andrew had ventured to disagree.

"How can you know, when it's thirty-five million miles away? How can we be sure unless we try?"

Von Plank had wheeled upon him.

"You know nothing!" he cried. "Any imbecile knows there is nothing on Mars!"

"Then why are we trying to go there?" put in one of the lab assistants.

Von Plank lost no time in demolishing him.

"Idiot! To beat the Russians! And we won't do it if we all gibble-gabble here. Back to work everyone, and clean out that mess. The results were negative, as I could have told Dr. Booth. I have read his report."

Von Plank ruled the laboratory with an iron hand. He would have reduced the time for lunch if it had not been defined in regulations. He followed carefully each assistant's work, peering over his shoulder and into his microscope, and no deviations for original research were allowed.

At first Andrew felt sorry for the German professor, who was obviously out of his environment among the easy going and friendly Americans. And it was apparent that he suffered from adenoids, or possibly sinus trouble, for he had a habit of snorting and breathing heavily with his mouth open as he examined the work of his underlings. The more he concentrated, the more his mouth dilated. But when he stood up to deliver his opinion—usually in the negative—it would clamp shut and his lips would be pressed into tight, uncompromising lines.

"What kind of a mess is this?" he would shout. "Keep your bench in better order!" Or, "Why have you not achieved a synthesis? You are proceeding very much too slowly!"

Andrew found that he soon forgot any sympathy for von Plank's ailments, if such they were. Probably psychosomatic, he told himself, when he heard the German breathing heavily down his neck and he steeled himself for the next biting criticism.

And so the occasional trip to the back of the lab and the quick look at the Mars jar became a kind of escape. When he thought he could detect something growing in the jar, he put it down at first to imagination. He wanted Dr. Booth's work to be recognized. He wanted von Plank to be confounded. It was funny what your imagination could do under the circumstances. Resolutely, he applied himself to the work in hand, determined to keep away from the corner with the jar, to forget all about it.

Nevertheless, when he went home that night and eight-year-old Howie climbed up in his lap, demanding to know what was new at the space project, Andrew found himself telling him about the jar. It made a good story. And when, after describing the work he ended with his observation that something *might* be growing there, the boy was wild with excitement.

"But Dad, they'll have to start the experiment again! Won't they?"

"No. Dr. Booth isn't here anymore and Dr. von Plank isn't interested."

"Oh, but they've got to! Can't you see, they've got to!" The child's mind jumped over all the doubts. "Dad, if they won't do it, couldn't you bring it home and let me watch it?"

"I'm afraid not, Howie. It's government property, you see. One of these days they'll clean it out like all the other jars."

"But they mustn't! They mustn't! I'd watch it so carefully! I would!"

Andrew realized that he had started one of those childish enthusiasms that could get out of hand.

"Look, son. I was just telling you a story. I don't think there's anything growing there at all. It only seemed like it, and I haven't had time to look carefully."

And you won't take time, either, he told himself. Can't let yourself get into a silly dither like the kid! Totally unscientific. And for the next week he applied himself doggedly to his scheduled work and didn't go near the back shelf. Every afternoon when he came home, Howie ran to meet him, demanding whether the mysterious plant in the jar had grown, and every time Andrew told him to stop being silly and forget about it.

And then one day he had to go into the back corner to look for a piece of apparatus, and almost against his will his eyes raised themselves to the top shelf and he looked at the jar. For a full minute he stood transfixed. There was no doubt about it this time. Something was growing in the jar. A flat, reddish brown lichen-like substance had covered the sand at the bottom, and several slender spikes were protruding upward from it.

Andrew stared, while his mind raced over all the possible explanations. The most obvious was that the jar was no longer airtight. Some foreign matter, some germ or spore or seed outside the experiment, had gotten in and was developing. He reached up and took down the jar, but after a close inspection, he admitted that it was airtight.

He must go back and reread Dr. Booth's notes. Which of the various seeds or spores had been in this jar? Which might now be growing, and were they developing in the usual manner, or was this something different? Something twisted by the alien environment?

His first reaction was to show this proof to Dr. von Plank, but he rejected the idea as soon as he thought of it. The *Herr Doktor* would be sure to follow his first negative impulse and throw the whole thing out, thus ruining any hope of a successful experiment. With his next thought, he remembered Howie's tearful insistence: "I'd watch it so carefully, I would!" Of course! He'd take it home to his own lab in his garage, and Howie could help him keep an eye on it. Who would miss an old jar that had been consigned to oblivion?

For the rest of the day, Andrew wrestled with the ethics of the situation, but by the time he went home, his mind was made up. The decision was somewhat simplified by the fact that his wife had gone to visit her sister and would not be there to exercise restraint. He ate with Howie in the base cafeteria and while he was putting the boy to bed, he explained about the jar. Howie was beside himself with excitement, and Andrew made a gesture toward child education by ordering him to have a place prepared for the jar on their lab bench by the time he got home the next day.

Andrew lived in one of the civilian houses nearest to the lab, and it was only a short walk to work. Next morning he took a large brown paper bag folded up in his briefcase, and it was a simple matter at the end of the day to slip the jar in the bag and walk out with it. Nobody asked any questions.

The Mars jar now sat in the place of honor in Andrew Elliott's little lab, and every morning and evening he and Howie rushed to see what changes had taken place in its contents. Andrew studied Dr. Booth's report and made an effort to set up the original temperature and light requirements.

They were not disappointed. Every day the growth within the jar increased. In a day or two, little round knobs appeared at the ends of the stalks.

"Just like antennae on insects!" cried Howie.

"Maybe we've got a Martian, Dad! Maybe that's how they communicate!"

"Nonsense!" said his father. "It's only some kind of vegetation. Wish I knew what had been planted in this jar." But all identifying marks had been removed in preparation for the cleaning, which it had somehow missed.

Andrew had promised himself that the Mars jar would be a secret between himself and his son, but he found it impossible to keep quiet about these exciting developments. Within a few days he had brought his best friends to see it, and soon it was the talk of the lab.

Dr. von Plank was the last one to hear of it, but hear it he did in a matter of days. He bore down upon Andrew, where he was concentrating on some figures, and the German's mouth was set in a tight, narrow line.

"What is this I hear about you, Dr. Elliott?" he snapped. "Absconding with government property! Setting up your own laboratory with equipment from the Army!"

"It's just one jar," Andrew protested. "Be glad to pay for it. Interests my boy, you know."

"I understand it interests more people than one boy. I understand it has an experiment in it, *Herr Doktor* Elliott. One of our experiments—filched from this project."

Andrew felt his blood pressure rising and tried to speak calmly.

"The experiment was finished, doctor. You remember, the Mars jars. You ordered it cleaned out. This one was left over, of no interest to anyone but the boy."

"Not convincing!" cried the German, his voice beginning to rise. "You are trying to make a monkey out of me, *Herr Doktor!* I see that! Now, you will bring back that jar and empty it before me. No, we will go together to your house and get it!"

"Now?" Andrew was aware of a sudden silence in the lab. All the scientists and assistants were listening. A kind of white-coated wall seemed to hem him in on every side, and von Plank and he were pitted against each other in the center. "But I'm right in the middle of some work now! I know—"

"You know nothing!" screamed von Plank. "Your work is of no importance. You will come with me now. That's an order!"

Andrew put down his notes and stood up. He felt the white-coated figures draw back to let him follow his chief from the room. His mind was running over a hundred possibilities and actions. In the lobby of the building he excused himself and ducked into the telephone booth.

Hoping that Howie might be home from school, he dialed his number and was relieved when the boy answered.

"Listen, son. I'm coming home now and Dr. von Plank is with me. Go down to the lab right away and hide the Mars jar. Hurry. And see if you can put something that looks like it in its place."

He came out of the booth, hoping his face did

not show deceit, trying to concoct an excuse for his superior. But the German was already out the door and down the walk. He had to run to catch up.

It was unfortunate that he lived so near the lab. Von Plank unerringly made for the garage door.

"Your lab is in here, I take it. Now if you'll open up for me, *Herr Doktor*."

Reluctantly, Andrew pulled open the door and followed the scientist inside. Howie stood at the table, the jar in his arms. He had not had time to make the substitution. As soon as he saw them, he began to cry.

"Don't let him take it, Dad! Don't let him open it up! He'll let them out. He'll let the Martians out and they'll all die!"

"So!" said von Plank. "A young scientist in the making, and he believes in Martians. This is government property, young man. It must go back to the project. Give it to me, please."

Even adults found it difficult to argue when the German spoke with the voice of authority. Howie handed over the jar, but his face seemed to crumple into the lines of childish frustration.

"Please don't let him out!" he cried. "I saw him, I really did. He waved at me. If you let him out, he'll die in our atmosphere. You'll kill him! You'll kill him!"

And then he choked and the tears came and he ran from the room.

"Well, well, you really have created an interest," said von Plank. "An interest in fairy tales. And now let's see what we have here." And he took the jar to the bench and sat down to examine it.

Suddenly, Andrew felt very tired of the whole business. Probably it was nothing more than an accidental anomaly over which he was risking his job and his career. It wasn't even his own experiment. And Howie was all worked up to an emotional crisis. This was no way to introduce the boy to science. With an exclamation of impatience, he turned and ran after his son, leaving von Plank alone in the lab.

He found the boy in his room and it took a good half hour to quiet him down, to get him to listen to reasonable arguments. But at last they were both able to go back downstairs with a certain appearance of calm. As they approached the garage, it struck Andrew that there was unexpected quiet in his lab. Had his superior simply taken the jar back to the project, leaving him to deal with the child? Perhaps the sensible thing to do.

They went into the garage and Andrew stopped in shocked silence at the scene before him. The jar lay overturned and open where his chief had dropped it, and paraphernalia from the work bench was scattered on the floor. Von Plank himself was sprawled across the table. Even before he went to investigate, there was no doubt in Andrew's mind. The wild contortion of the limbs, the discolored face told him that the scientist was dead. As he stood immobilized by surprise and horror, Howie pushed past him, shrilly crying his appraisal of the situation.

"It killed him, Dad! Look there! He let the Martian out and it killed him!"

Late that night, Andrew was still living in a state of shock and disbelief as he waited in the office of Army Intelligence for the autopsy report. Events, he felt, were closing in on him. The officer had refused to let him go home to take care of Howie, who was now sleeping at a neighbor's. Patiently and politely, for he was a civilian scientist, to be treated with respect, they had gone over the events of the day.

Over and over. His relations with the German had not been the most amicable, had they? It was true that he took a piece of equipment from the lab? Everyone on the project had given a vivid description of the argument that ensued. And afterwards, in his garage; how could he explain the angry shouts reported by the neighbors. Some even said the child was crying, "You'll kill him!"

Murder! They hadn't charged him with it yet, but it was obvious what they thought. How had he come to this appalling situation? From the innocent observation of a discarded jar? Perhaps he should never have taken it home, but many men spirited more valuable things from the lab than a disused jar. Now his job was in jeopardy—his career, perhaps even his life!

Andrew tried vainly to sort it all out. Von Plank was hard to get along with. Anyone would testify to that. But murder! Could he be losing his mind? Some kind of blackout? He saw again the wild disorder in his garage. What could have happened to the man? His imagination raced with fantasies of science fiction: an extraterrestrial menace, a lethal Martian miasma that escaped from the jar to overwhelm the professor. With an effort at sanity, he raised his head and looked at the colonel.

"Why can't you believe my son? I know he's only a child, but he won't lie to you. We both left the man in perfect health. I was upstairs with Howard for half an hour."

"Yes, I know. We've talked to the boy. You'll excuse me if I say he seems a bit—um, fanciful. He insists a Martian did it."

"I've told you that's because of the experiment. Dr. Booth's experiment. This was an old jar. It interested both me and the boy."

The colonel sighed.

"Yes, I know," he said again. "But I'm afraid you'll have to come up with a better explanation than that." He wished the doctor would hurry with the autopsy. What wouldn't these scientists dream up next!

At last the door opened and the young medical officer entered and laid his report before the colonel. That officer stared at it.

"Does this make sense, Doc?"

"I doubt it. But that's what it was. He was asphyxiated by a seed in his windpipe."

Andrew was on his feet. "A seed!"

The officers looked at him in surprise.

"Seem reasonable to you?" the colonel demanded.

With a flash of insight, Andrew saw what must have happened. Those little bulbs on the ends of the stalks, they were seed pods! He saw von Plank bending over, intent upon the jar, his wheezing mouth open, as it did when he was concentrating. He saw him break the seal and lift the lid and the resulting implosion of the near vacuum give wings to the seed, which with the plant's last effort at self propagation flew out of the Mars jar and down von Plank's throat, causing him to drop the jar and almost demolish the lab as he struggled frantically for breath.

As simply as possible, Andrew explained his theory to the two men. They looked at each other and shook their heads.

"It's the only thing that fits, that's certain," said the medical officer.

"The kid was right after all," the colonel admitted. "The jar killed him. What a freak accident!" He was relieved that he would not be involved in a murder investigation after all. "You'd better go home to your boy, Dr. Elliott. He needs you. Just be around when we want you for the inquest."

Andrew mumbled his thanks and rose to go, hardly believing that the nightmare was over. At the door he paused and turned uncertainly.

"Just one thing, doctor. Could I—could you, when you're done with it, let me have the seed?"

"The seed? You want the damned seed?"

"Yes. You see, it's very important to me to find out what it is."

"Oh. Well, all right, professor. We'll save it for you."

They watched him make his way out the door and then the colonel brought his fist down on the desk.

"Isn't that just like a scientist? Inhuman."

29557 JOHNNY/BINGO, by Browning Norton. Kidnapped by ruthless bank robbers, two thirteen-year-old boys carry out a bold plan of escape. (75¢)

29523 THE TERRIBLE CHURNADRYNE, by Eleanor Cameron. Illustrated by Beth and Joe Krush. A strange and terrifying creature stalks Jennifer and Tom as they are returning home through the fog at dusk. (75¢)

29579 BASKETBALL TALK, by Howard Liss. Illustrated by Frank Robbins. Here is a dictionary that gives you the A to Z on the fundamentals of America's most popular team sport so you can follow the fast, exciting action on the court. (75¢)

29707 JACKIE ROBINSON OF THE BROOKLYN DODGERS, by Milton J. Shapiro. Illustrated with photographs. The courageous black man who broke the color line in professional baseball and became one of the all-time greats of the Brooklyn Dodgers. (95¢)

29577 THREE ON THE RUN, by Nina Bawden. Frontispiece illustration by Wendy Worth. Sudden adventure grips Ben, Lil, and their African friend, Thomas Okapi, as they are plunged into an international plot and must make a wild, desperate flight from London. (75¢)

29546 DRUGS AND YOU, by Arnold Madison. Illustrated with photographs. This straightforward account gives you basic information about the use and abuse of today's major drugs. (75¢)

29526 ALVIN FERNALD, FOREIGN TRADER, by Clifford B. Hicks. Illustrated by Bill Sokol. Alvin goes on a glorious but zany trip to Europe and gets involved with industrial spies. (75¢)

29327 PERPLEXING PUZZLES AND TANTALIZING TEASERS, by Martin Gardner. Illustrated by Laszlo Kubinyi. A fascinating collection of puzzles and teasers to challenge your wits, tickle your funny bone, and give you and your friends hours of entertainment. (60¢)

29311 LITTLE VIC, by Doris Gates. Illustrated by Kate Seredy. A young man's courageous struggle to qualify as a jockey and to ride the horse he loves to victory. (60¢)

29581 FOOTBALL TALK, by Howard Liss. Illustrated by Frank Robbins. Here is a dictionary that gives you the A to Z on the basic rules and strategy of the game so you can enjoy the fast action and split-second decisions that take place on the gridiron. (75¢)

75843